Gun In Hand . . .

Carter hid in the shadows, his presence unsuspected by Anis—Koulami's woman. The deadly seductress knocked on the hotel room door.

As the door opened, Carter moved. He grabbed Anis and crashed into the room. Inside were three men. Three Walther PPKs popped into their hands.

Carter held his Luger to Anis' head. "Looks like a stalemate."

Koulami didn't think so. He fired point blank into his woman. A slug ripped through her, hitting Carter. He went down . . .

NICK CARTER IS IT!

FROM THE NICK CARTER KILLMASTER SERIES

NICK CARTER

KILLMASTER

Slaughter Day

C

CHARTER BOOKS, NEW YORK

Dedicated to the men of the
Secret Services of the
United States of America

SLAUGHTER DAY

A Charter Book/published by arrangement with
The Condé Nast Publications, Inc.

PRINTING HISTORY
Charter edition/October 1986

ISBN: 0-441-57287-1

Charter Books are published by The Berkley Publishing Group,
200 Madison Avenue, New York, New York 10016.
PRINTED IN THE UNITED STATES OF AMERICA

ONE

Dusk had fallen and the promise of a darker night hung in the clouds. Carter drove slowly, checking the brass numbers on the gates. When he found the one he wanted, he sped up.

Two blocks farther on, he pulled into a closed filling station and parked. Before getting out, he checked the loads in Wilhelmina, his 9mm Luger, and screwed a four-inch silencer into the barrel.

With the gun comfortably back in its shoulder rig, he stepped from the car and locked it.

He was in the Polo district outside Marseille. The houses were small, spaced wide apart, with whitewashed walls around them and generally well-tended lawns and gardens. It wasn't an affluent area, but neither were the people who lived there poor.

Most of them were Moroccan and Algerian middle class, small-time shopkeepers and blue-collar workers.

He walked back the two blocks, passed the house, and moved down an alley to the rear. The narrow wooden gate in the wall was unlocked. Carter slipped into the garden and closed it silently behind him.

There was a light on in the kitchen. Inside, Carter could see Allad Khopar moving around preparing a meal. The man was dark, grossly overweight, and bald. In appearance and background, Khopar fit the neighborhood. Similarities ended there. If he'd wanted to, he could have lived in one of the elaborate mansions in the hills north of Marseille.

The man was rich.

He was a supplier. If someone wanted to go to Cairo, or London, or Rome, or practically any city in the world to make a kill, Khopar would have the gun they would need waiting for them when they got there.

If a particular group wanted to blow up something, or someone, Khopar could supply their choice of explosive—Quarrex, Togel, Polar Gelignite, even Gelemax.

There wasn't a thing in the world Khopar couldn't obtain for a price. And all of his customers were terrorists.

Carter filled his hand with the Luger and rapped lightly on the door. He heard a cup and saucer rattle, and then the man's voice.

"Who's there?"

"Jalar sent me," Carter murmured.

"I don't do business at the house" came the reply. "See me at the warehouse in the morning."

"This is an emergency."

There was a mumbled curse in Arabic and French from the other side of the door, and the lock turned.

The moment Carter saw light, he shoved. The door slammed into Khopar's fat gut and sent him down flat on his ass. Carter stuck Wilhelmina up the man's nose and heeled the door shut.

"What is this? Who are you?" the man gasped.

"The name's not important, Khopar, but this is. I want information. Lots of it."

"Get out!"

He tried to struggle to his feet. Carter raised the Luger and brought the barrel down across the man's collarbone, breaking it with a sickening crunch.

Khopar went back down with a wail of pain and his eyes flew wide with fear. "Who are you . . . ?"

"Your runner, Jalar, is dead."

"You?"

"That's right, pig, so you know I'm bad."

"What do you want?"

"Amin Koulami. The Puppet Master."

Khopar lay on the tiled floor with his left arm hanging limp, and choked. "You're mad!"

"A lot of people are," Carter hissed, and moved the muzzle downward. "I think I'll blow off your kneecaps before I kill you."

"No, no! I . . . I don't know any Koulami."

"Bullshit! We've been on you for weeks. A month ago two exiled Iranian businessmen were cut down in San Francisco with a specially rigged Mannlicter single-action CD-13. You supplied the gun and the loads. A week ago in Paris, another Iranian, the head of an antigovernment faction, was gassed along with his family. The weapon was a hermetically sealed six-inch aluminum tube. It fired liquid poison. You supplied the gun and the gas pellets."

"No . . ."

Carter spotted a lit cigar smoldering in an ashtray. There was a humidor of fresh ones nearby. He picked up the lit cigar and used it to light a second one from the humidor.

Khopar lay motionless as Carter puffed until the ends

of both cigars were cherry red. Then he returned to the fear-filled man and squatted.

"Koulami is the worst kind of terrorist. He's as fanatical as the crazy imams he works for, and he's suicidal to boot. He's set up cells all over Europe with nuts like himself. He calls them puppets, and he's their puppet master. Are you listening, Khopar?"

"Y-y-yesss."

"And you, for a price, supply them. Now, I know that in the next few days something big is going down. I want Koulami before that happens."

"He . . . he would kill me."

"I'll kill you," Carter growled. "But not before I stuff these cigars in your ears and break your other collarbone. And that will be just for openers. It could be a very long night, Khopar."

The man's Adam's apple quaked as he swallowed. His wide eyes never left the cigars, and his voice was raspy with fear when he spoke.

"I've never met him, never even seen him."

"How do you make contact?"

"A dead drop in Paris. I get a phone call. Jalar flies up and picks up the order. We fill it, and pick up payment from the same drop."

"And you've never made face-to-face contact?"

"Never, I swear it!" The man's jowls were quivering and his cheeks were pale, shiny with a film of sweat.

"How do you reach them in an emergency?"

There was a silent pause. It radioed the fact that the man was going to lie. "I don't. They only contact me."

Carter didn't speak. He stabbed the cigars out on the floor, one on each side of Khopar's head.

"Put an ad in the *Tribune*!" the man cried at once.

"The night the ad comes out, go to the Club Marie. The upstairs women's lounge. The tank of the booth against the windows. Use an oilskin bag."

"What's the wording in the ad?"

" 'Allah is great, Allah is wonderful, Allah is merciful to us all.' Sign it, Mennenamah."

"Sit up!"

"Wh-what are you going to do? My God, I told you what you wanted to know. You're not—"

Carter curled his arm around the man's neck. When he was sure he had the carotid artery, he squeezed.

It took only seconds.

He dropped him back to the tile, took a pound of pure heroin from his jacket, and put it on the table.

Outside, he crossed the street to a black Renault sedan. Inside were two solid, solemn types. They didn't glance up at him when Carter leaned against the side of the car.

"The junk is on the table. He's out on the kitchen floor. Can you hold him for at least a week?"

"At least," replied one of the narcotics squad officers. "Probably longer."

"Tell the SDECE boys thanks for me. A week should be plenty long enough."

Carter strolled back to his car. By the time he pulled out, both men had already left the Renault and disappeared around the corner of Khopar's house.

Carter requested and got a seat in the rear of the first-class section of the Air France 727. The hop from Marseille to Paris would be short, an hour, but he didn't feel like exchanging recipes with some sweet old dowager from Chantilly.

"Would you care for a drink, monsieur?"

The stewardess looked exactly like French women are supposed to look: sleek, trim, dark hair, high cheekbones, yet curves where curves are supposed to be.

In short, a thoroughbred.

"Scotch, one cube. Chivas if you have it."

"*Oui, monsieur.*"

The liftoff was smooth, and even before the No Smoking sign went off, she arrived with two miniatures and a glass with one large cube on a tray.

"*Monsieur.*"

"*Merci.*"

Carter let his eyes scan her attractive cleavage as she leaned over to set the tray and pour the drink.

"Did monsieur have a profitable day in Marseille?"

Then Carter remembered. She had also been on the morning flight down from Paris. He hadn't paid much attention then. His mind had been full of Khopar.

"Pretty boring, really. Everyday stuff. But I'm looking forward to a day or two of relaxation in Paris."

Their eyes met, and to Carter's surprise, a charming blush colored her cheeks. He also thought he saw invitation, or even a challenge, in her eyes.

He didn't know it, but she had already told the other two stewardesses that this one was "hers." She smiled again. Carter smiled and lit a cigarette, realizing that there were some small encounters that almost made constant travel worthwhile.

As top agent and sometime executioner for supersecret AXE, Nick Carter, N3, did more traveling than most airline captains.

He had been on this one since the day, a month earlier, the two Iranians had gotten themselves snuffed in San Francisco. Until that time, the FBI had followed suspects domestically, and the CIA had looked under rocks abroad in this most recent organized round of terror.

Ordinarily, if the nuts, the radicals, and general bad boys kept their killing in their own backyards, American intelligence watched but kept hands off.

But when they started doing their hits on U.S. soil, that—as the saying goes—was the straw that broke the camel's back.

David Hawk, the cigar-chomping, gruff-mannered head of AXE, had not minced words.

"The Langley boys are ninety-nine percent sure that this Amin Koulami is behind it. He calls himself 'the Puppet Master.' Go after him, Nick, and get the son of a bitch."

So Carter went after him, turning over his own rocks, rousting his own snitches, and swapping fists and lies with lowlifes from Beirut to Munich to Rome to Tangier.

It had taken a long time to sniff out the trail to Khopar. Now he had a line on the Puppet Master himself, and he planned to use it.

"Another drink, monsieur?"

"No, this is fine. *Merci.*"

She returned to the galley, and Carter, watching her move, decided she was a ten from the back as well as the front.

He leaned back, loosened his tie, and let his thoughts drift to his quarry.

As a youth, Amin Koulami had been weaned on radical terrorism during the reign of the Shah of Iran. He had made his first bones at the age of twelve by taking out four SAVAK agents in their car with a dynamite bomb.

By the age of sixteen he was a trained and seasoned killer, having taken his apprenticeship in munitions, hand-to-hand, and general terror tactics in Syria and Lebanon.

By the time he was in his twenties, Koulami was a recognized leader and the Shah was gone. Since the revolution, he had carried out the wishes of the new regime on a worldwide basis.

In the last year or so, he had traveled all over the world organizing highly complex cells. The men and women he had recruited as followers were as fanatical as he was.

For a long time the puppets and their master had dabbled in basic assassination and general terrorism. In the last month, while Carter had hunted, he had turned up a lot of evidence that Koulami and company were gearing up for something big and much more direct than a few random hits.

The Killmaster meant to find out what that something big was and snuff it, as well as Koulami.

The seat belt light came on in preparation for landing at Charles de Gaulle. Carter was busy strapping himself in when the familiar voice was right at his ear.

"May I join you for the landing, Monsieur Carter?" she asked with an even more enchanting smile than the last one.

"Only if you call me Nick," he said with a grin.

When she sat down, her skirt slid well above her knees. As she buckled up, she didn't bother to tug it down.

"I am Stephanie. You are on business in Paris?"

"Nothing that's going to take up all my time. Do you live in Paris?"

"No, I share a flat with my sister several miles outside Paris. It is a long train ride after flying all day."

"I imagine you often stay in the city."

"Often, if I can find the proper accommodations," she said.

"Will mine do? I'm at the Ritz."

"I adore the Ritz."

Stephanie Riquet was a woman who knew her own mind. When she saw something she wanted, she promptly went after it. In this case, what she wanted was Carter.

And the Killmaster didn't mind at all. It would be a very interesting evening. It would take the boredom out of the Paris wait, and when the time came, it would be much easier for Stephanie to plant the message in the ladies' lounge than trying to do it himself.

The black Mercedes and the driver assigned to him by AXE Paris awaited them in the limousine area.

The driver was Charles LeMoine. He was a large man, with blond hair, blue eyes, a military manner, and a beautifully tailored suit. He said nothing to Carter, but a sly smile tickled the corners of his mouth when the Killmaster helped the beautiful stewardess into the rear of the Mercedes.

When they were settled into the luxurious glove leather seats, she turned to Carter. "You have your own car and driver?"

"A perk provided by my company," he replied.

"Who do you work for?" she asked, wide-eyed.

"A company that specializes in cleaning up the environment." The car pulled from the curb and maneuvered smoothly through traffic. "Did you get the ad in, Charley?"

"Yes, sir. It will be in the morning *Trib*."

"Good."

"The Ritz?"

"Yeah, Charley, and that will be it for the night."

Another smile at Carter in the rearview mirror. "You bet."

Carter knew what was going through the young driver's mind: *Field agents . . . the bastards get all the action!*

A half hour later the big car pulled silently up to the entrance of the hotel. Carter passed both his and the woman's bag to a waiting bellman.

"We checked in yesterday . . . Suite Seven-ten."

"Oui, monsieur."

The elevator was crowded. Carter put his arm around Stephanie and pulled her to him to take up less space.

She smiled, and then suddenly frowned. Carter thought he knew why, and was already formulating answers to her questions in his mind.

In the suite, he tipped the bellman and built them both drinks from the mini-bar.

They both felt tired and grimy from the flight and the long day, and said so with just their eyes.

Stephanie took her travel bag and disappeared into the bath without a word. After a few minutes, when she had the shower going full blast, Carter joined her.

"One question?"

"Sure."

"I'm not the brightest girl in the world, but I could swear that was a gun I felt under your jacket in the elevator."

"It was."

"Why does an environmental protectionist carry a gun?"

Carter shrugged. "Sometimes the environment gets a little rough."

"But—"

"Shhh. That was your one question."

He took her in his arms and kissed her before she got too inquisitive.

Minutes later, still wet, they hurried from the bath to the bed. Carter threw the quilt down and they both dived under the sheet.

"Do you think I am wanton?" Stephanie giggled, throwing a naked leg over his body.

"Yes," Carter replied, pulling her to him and feeling the fullness of her breasts pillow across his chest.

She kissed his neck below the ear and let her lips travel over his cheek to his. At the same time, her hand ran under the sheet, found him, and began to excite him almost unbearably with the feathering touch of her long red nails.

The kiss ended, but their lips lingered, just touching. Carter ran his hand down her back and across the bare leg still draped over him.

He heard her moan and felt her snuggle closer to him. Then her soft hand grew more urgent, caressing him fiercely.

Her breasts were marvelous, perfectly formed, and responsive to his lips. The nipples swelled beneath the teasing of his tongue.

"Oh, yes . . . good, so good."

Slowly, with care, he slid his hand over the gentle rise of her belly. Her thighs parted and his fingers found her.

She shivered and began to breathe faster. Her fingers left him and snaked up, around his neck. Her breasts pressed harder against his lips and her thighs molded to his.

Clasping her by the buttocks, Carter drew her even closer. He kissed her hungrily, now thrusting his tongue deep into her sweet, willing mouth.

She moaned in pleasure, the sound an animal growl deep in her throat. Her teeth nicked his lower lip. She rolled her body expertly while her arms clutched tighter and her fingers dug into his flesh.

Then he was between her thighs, taking her, both of them reveling in the coupling. Beneath him the woman lay panting quietly, pulsing internally around him.

When their explosion came it was violent, mutual, and then they fell apart, gasping, not speaking.

They rested like that for several moments. Eventually she sat up in the bed, completely at ease in her nudity before him.

"I'm off tomorrow."

Carter smiled. "I suspected you might be. Are you hungry now?"

"Famished."

"We'll order up."

"And then?"

"Back to bed, of course." He laughed. "Uh, Stephanie, tomorrow evening . . ."

"Yes?"

"There's a little favor I'd like to ask of you . . ."

TWO

There were fifteen tourists in the three o'clock tour of the Tennessee Atomic and Space Development Authority. They came in all shapes and sizes and ranged in age from sixteen to sixty.

A few were attentive. Some were merely interested. Others were downright bored.

One, a woman, was rapt.

She was in her late twenties, and had the kind of beauty one sees staring from the covers of fashion magazines or selling cosmetics on television. Her hair was a deep brown with reddish highlights and caught up in an intricate knot at the nape of her slender neck. The eyes, full of intelligence, were large and as dark as her hair. Her clothes, like her face, projected a smooth sophistication.

She looked Latin, and when she spoke, her carefully modulated voice had just the trace of an accent. But not even a language expert could recognize her native language. Her English was perfect, honed by years of university study in England and the United States.

Her name was Selwa Rajon, and she had been born

twenty-eight years before in Tehran, Iran. Since the age of twelve she had been a confirmed revolutionary. Off and on since her thirteenth birthday, she had been the mistress of Amin Koulami.

Behind the glass before her she saw Dr. Hubert Einmetz guide the delicate equipment used to open a four-foot-square concrete storage vault.

Einmetz had devoted his entire adult life to atomic research. He was considered a top authority in the field of plutonium: its manufacture, storage, and movement. In the Tennessee facility, he was in charge of final inspection and shipment of the potentially lethal product.

As Einmetz guided two mechanical claws into the vault and extracted a long metallic cylinder, the tour guide began his spiel.

"Ladies and gentlemen, what you see is pure plutonium. If we were exposed to its radioactivity for little more than a second, it would kill us."

Selwa Rajon could hardly keep her hands still or her lower lip from trembling as she watched the cylinder being placed on a scale by the scientist.

"Plutonium has two characteristics: its radioactive properties, and its fissionable elements. The only use for these elements, in their pure form, is in the making of an atomic or hydrogen bomb."

"Are we safe here?" asked the youngest member of the group, a teen-age girl.

"Quite. There are warning devices all over the complex that would warn us immediately if there were the slightest trace of leakage."

An older man said, "Is there enough plutonium in that cylinder to make a bomb?"

"As you can see from the scale, the cylinder Dr. Einmetz is weighing is exactly twelve pounds. That would be about half the plutonium needed to construct a weapon. It takes about twenty-two or twenty-three pounds to create a critical mass which will explode without any alternate assistance. That is why the plutonium is stored in cylinders of twelve pounds. In this weight mass—under twenty-two pounds—the plutonium is safe and cannot explode.''

Selwa spoke. ''Are the containers he is shifting now going to storage?''

''No, they are part of a shipment. Now, if you will all follow me . . .''

As they filed past the glass, the woman narrowed her eyes to examine the side of the cushioned crates into which the cylinders were being loaded.

She smiled when she saw the present day's date on them.

The moon was in the first quarter, pale gold over the valley. There was a high overcast, and scudding clouds kept blotting out the moonlight.

Four figures, all in skintight black ski suits, worked diligently in the center of the narrow, winding mountain road. They worked in teams of two, about sixty yards from each other. In each team, one man would dig with pickax and shovel while the other stood by holding a Russian-made T52 land mine.

The T52 is shaped like a woman's purse compact. It is about eighteen inches in diameter, five inches deep at the center, and armed by a pressure device.

It is also powerful. An ordinary car will disintegrate with the blast from one mine.

Each man carried an AR-12 slung over his shoulder and a belt at his waist containing a U.S. army-issue .45 and a walkie-talkie.

The holes were dug and the two devices were placed. All four men carefully covered them.

They were barely finished when the walkies at their belts came to life. "Mars, this is Jupiter. Do you read?" It was a woman's voice.

"Loud and clear," replied the largest of the four men, his English thickly accented.

"How close are you?"

"Finished."

"Good. They are through the gate and on the way," the woman said.

"As usual?"

"Yes. A jeep heading with four soldiers, all armed. Thirty yards back, the armored truck. One driver, one passenger, both armed. Behind the truck, a sedan with three uniformed men and one civilian."

"We'll be ready."

The four men moved to a prearranged position. Two climbed the hill above the road. They hunkered down and began assembling a Russian RPG-7 rocket launcher.

The RPG-7 was an ideal weapon for the use it would be put to this night. It was recoilless and equipped with an infrared telescopic scope for night sighting. It was capable of putting a very large hole in a tank, let alone the flimsy skin of an ordinary car.

While the first man slung the RPG-7 to his shoulder, the second sighted in the scope of his Armalite.

Before the other two men left the road, they attached incendiaries to both of the mines. They then ran fuses up the back ten feet or so and attached them to short trees.

This done, they climbed down the slope and hid themselves behind a mound of large rocks. Both men unslung their Armalites, sighted them in on the center of the road, and waited.

Minutes later they heard the vehicles climbing the

long grade in low gear. First the headlights' glare came into view, and then the lead jeep.

All four men lying in wait tensed, ready. The vehicles seemed to be crawling. Then they heard the gears shift and the lead jeep spurted ahead.

The jeep's right front wheel set off the T52. A brilliant flash of white quickly turned to orange as the incendiaries went off a millisecond later. The mine's blast lifted the jeep and its occupants several feet into the air.

The force of the blast had been outward, away from the hill, throwing the jeep toward the ravine. It came down on its nose on the shoulder of the road and then rolled on down the mountain.

It was like daylight around the remaining two vehicles. The RPG man on the hill balanced the scope sight against his forehead and fired.

There was a great *whoosh* as flaming gas shot from the launcher's rear. The grenade itself flew from the barrel, its fins opening as soon as it was clear.

The distance from the shooter on the hill was 150 yards. The rocket found its mark in one second. It made a small hole in the side of the sedan. The crash-sensitive fuse set off the main detonator right behind it in the main shell.

Tiny fragments of steel exploded throughout the sedan, shredding the four bodies inside.

In the glare of the incendiaries, the firing from the Armalites was pinpoint accurate and deadly. All six tires were shot out two seconds after the initial mine blast. Before driver or guard could find the armored truck's firing slots with the muzzles of their machine pistols or rub the glare of the blast from their eyes, a black figure appeared in front of them.

It was the man with the RPG-7. A second rocket hissed from its muzzle and penetrated the bulletproof windshield like a knife slicing butter.

The screams of the driver and guard had barely died out before the two men were at the rear doors. One held a power pack while the other cut a neat hole around the lock and handle with a laser torch.

By the time Selwa Rajon arrived with a panel truck, all the cylinders of plutonium had been carried from the armored vehicles.

"Any survivors?" she asked.

"None."

"Excellent. How many cylinders?"

White teeth gleamed in the man's dark face. "Enough to make two very fat bombs."

About five miles outside the town of Worthing, in the county of Sussex in southern England, is the former estate of the Earl of Tremont. It was—and is—a grand old estate that only the Crown or a very eccentric American billionaire could afford to keep up.

Hating the crude Americans, Lord Tremont ten years ago sold the estate to the British government for enough money to allow himself, his wife, and his mistress to live comfortably in Marbella, Spain.

Within a year after its sale, the estate was converted into a think tank and storage place for England's atomic energy research. Its basements were made into vaults, and an elaborate security system was installed.

Armed guards were always on duty, but the shifts usually required only five men. After all, the only things stored there were computer records and other paper work.

The large formal drawing room had been converted into a common room and general canteen. On this night, four men sipped tea and awaited their watch. The men they would relieve were stationed around the estate. Two men patrolled the grounds on foot, a third was stationed in the computer room upstairs monitoring the alarm system, and the fourth lolled in a chair outside the vault room.

Corporals Clary and Fitzmorris were the walking guards on the grounds. They heard the sound, but before they could bring their Sten guns into play, their throats were cut. They were dead before they hit the ground.

In the computer room, Sergeant Hadley Wells came out of his seat as all the television screens monitoring the house and grounds went black.

"Bloody things," he hissed, and reached for the in-house phone.

On this bitter cold night a coal fire burned in the common room. In a smaller, adjoining room—once the master's study and now the off-duty sleeping quarters for the watch—Linus Baker growled and reached for the phone.

"Baker here. What is it?"

"Wells . . ."

"I've a half hour yet, you bloody twit."

"I know that. Before you come up, check the master cable. The tellies have gone off again."

Baker groaned. "Probably more bloody seepage. They put 'em too near the rain drains."

"Just check the cutoffs, would you?"

Baker pulled on a heavy windbreaker and left by the rear door. Stairs behind it led down to a rear exit from the house.

A biting wind hit him in the face the moment he opened the door and walked into the courtyard. He heard nothing of the soft-soled shoes that stepped from the darkness behind him. He had no premonition of danger as he bent over the cable box and fished in his pocket for his keys.

"Blimey, the bloody padlock's gone!" he muttered.

Death was instantaneous as a single 9mm slug, fired single-shot from a silenced Walther, drove into the back of his skull.

"Is he dead?"

"Very."

"Get the keys."

Four men in black clothing with darkened faces moved up the rear stairs. As they ran, they donned gas masks and adjusted the tanks on their backs.

They went through the small sleeping area without a pause and burst into the common room.

The four men looked up in total surprise. Not one of them moved to save himself as the deadly cyanide gas hit each of them full in the face.

The four attackers hardly paused. Two of them went up the main staircase and ran down the hall to the computer room. The other two went down the stairs to the cellars.

A long narrow hall led them to the vault anteroom. Through the small pane in the door they could see the guard. He sat at a small table reading the *Times*. Behind him was the steel door to the main vault.

The two men paused. One took a walkie from the belt at his waist while the other packed the crack around the door's latch and lock with C-4 explosive.

"Mogalli?"

"Yes" came the reply from the walkie-talkie.

"We are there."

On the second floor, the man named Mogalli barked "Wait!" into his walkie and nodded to his comrade.

The man used the keys he had taken from the dead hand of Linus Baker.

Inside, Sergeant Hadley Wells sighed with anger. Baker was relieving him, and the goddamned tellies were still out. He would have to check the cables himself.

As the door opened, he swung around in his swivel chair. "Baker, what the hell—"

Two slugs ripped through his chest, rupturing Sergeant Hadley Wells's heart before he even saw his killers.

"Go back down and reconnect the power cable!"

"Yes, Mogalli."

As his comrade scurried from the room, the man called Mogalli again pressed the button on his walkie. "Mustafa, go!"

In the cellars below, the anteroom door exploded from its hinges. The guard inside was blown from his chair against the wall.

Dimly, through the haze of smoke before him and the tears in his eyes, he saw two dark figures enter the room.

He managed to claw the Webley halfway from its holster before he was pinned harder against the wall by double bursts of machine gun fire.

The man called Mustafa shoved the body from in front of the vault door and went about his work without a wasted motion.

He packed the whole door with C-4, jammed a detonator into the doughy explosive, and ran back down the hallway, closely followed by his comrade.

It was a twenty-second fuse and absolutely precise. The blast reverberated through the entire house, and within seconds after it had died out, both men were going through the file drawers in the vault.

They worked with purpose, ignoring everything that didn't pertain to their needs.

By the time they entered the second-floor computer room twenty minutes later with the computer access codes, the man called Mogalli had already powered up the computers.

"Excellent," he hissed, already letting his stubby fingers fly over the keys of the computer.

Within a half hour the printer was clacking away, spilling out the newly refined processing plans for the cooling and refining of nuclear waste into raw plutonium.

Mogalli, through an excellent knowledge of computers and an uncanny sense for search, had also been able to come up with two plus factors.

He had obtained the shipping codes and access numbers needed to hook up with the computers of one of the world's largest producers of raw uranium in the Lake Athabasca region of northern Saskatchewan.

And from the center's personnel file he had obtained the current status and location of the world-renowned nuclear physicist, Dr. Josef Brussman.

Morgan Pawley could hardly believe his luck. He had taken his weekly trip up to Bombay to convince his bankers and other creditors to hold off foreclosure for a little while longer.

As usual, they had screamed and shouted and finally agreed to let Pawley continue to run his air service a while longer.

After leaving them, he made the usual rounds of the big hotels, trying to scrounge up a little business.

"Got a Beechcraft six-passenger. I usually charter, but I do one-day sightseeing hops as well. No? How about a helicopter ride? I've got a Bell that seats six, with cargo room. See Bombay from the air. My airfield is only a few minutes' drive south of Bombay, at Calapa Point . . .''

He hit five hotels and got no takers.

And then, in the Hilton lounge, he met her. She said her name was Rami. He never caught her last name and couldn't have cared less.

She said she was Lebanese, a refugee from the Beirut mess. She lived now with her rich aunt and uncle in London. She was vacationing with her aunt and was bored. Auntie had already gone to sleep up in the suite, so Rami had decided to come down to the lounge for a drink and a little fun.

Yes, she would adore a helicopter ride over Bombay at night. It would be romantic.

Pawley had driven like a madman back to the field. He had tried to steer her into bed without the helicopter ride, but she would have none of it.

Up they went and she had loved it. And she had been the most inquisitive passenger he had ever had, asking a million and one questions.

Where did he store his fuel? What were his clearance signals? Did he know of Trapur, north of Bombay? What were the little village's coordinates? Where did he store his charts?

He had answered everything without thinking why she asked.

He was much more interested in the wealth of her body under the chic jump suit she wore.

Pawley had been born and raised and damned near died a couple of times in India. He had inherited the flying service from an alcoholic uncle ten years earlier, along with all its debts. At the time, Pawley had been in London getting by as best he could with a little smuggling and gunrunning for mercs going to Africa.

The uncle's death came at a perfect time for him to return to India. He was on his way to jail in England.

"Thank you so much for the ride," she said, moving into the living room of his apartment over the ramshackle hangar.

"Do you really have to go back to Bombay tonight?" Pawley asked, watching her move into the room in front of him.

She moved like an oiled machine inside the jump suit. Pawley could feel an ache in his groin as he imagined her long, smooth body. Her dark hair gleamed like silk and her almond-shaped eyes, when she glanced over her shoulder to reply, seemed to flame with a promise of uninhibited passion.

"Oh, yes, I do have to return to the hotel. But not before dawn."

Ah, Pawley, you lucky bugger, you won't have to dig into your bloody kick for one of Madame Kohler's used-up whores tonight!

"Would you like a drink?"

"No. I think we have drunk enough tonight, don't you?"

"Ah, yes, lass, that we have."

Her fingers barely seemed to move. They did something to the snaps at her neck, then he heard the zipper. Suddenly the jump suit was puddled around her feet and she wasn't wearing a thing beneath it.

"Jesus," Pawley gasped, ripping at his own shirt and throwing it aside.

She was a beautiful, totally sexual creature. Her breasts were large and firm and showed slightly blue where the veins ran into the dark nipples. Her hips were wide and tapered down perfectly to her long, tanned legs.

Rami Sherif breathed deeply, expanding her voluptuousness, drawing him to her as the flame draws the moth.

He came willingly, like a lamb led by the Judas goat to the slaughter. As he moved, he dropped his pants and nearly stumbled before he could kick them away.

Her waist-length hair was held by a barrette at the back of her neck. As he dropped to his knees and slobbered at her breasts, Rami undid the barrette. She shook out her hair and then leaned forward, letting its glossy fullness fall across his back.

"Beautiful, beautiful," he groaned, letting his lips trail down across her belly as her nails worked their way up his back to his neck and throat.

He heard a tiny crack, like a glass breaking, but paid no attention as the musk from her body filled his nostrils.

Rami Sherif smiled. She was enjoying this. She loved to have men slobber and fawn over her. But only one man had ever truly claimed her.

Amin Koulami.

She shook the broken glass free from the needle and jammed it into Pawley's neck.

The cyanide worked in seconds. When his body released her and slipped to the floor, she stepped over it and headed for his closet. Along the way she checked her watch.

She had plenty of time, four hours at least, before the raid started. In the helicopter she would reach the nuclear power station in Trapur in just over an hour.

THREE

Carter tried not to think about his misgivings in using a civilian for this. He could easily have used one of the AXE agents from the Paris office. But there was something about Stephanie Riquet, an innocence and charm, that gave her the perfect cover. She looked and acted like exactly what she was, a civilian.

And before the night was over, that fact might save both their skins.

He had spent the day, after leaving her, conferring with Washington and the local SDECE. The French wanted Koulami as much as AXE and Carter did. They would, however, have to handle him with kid gloves. Carter had no such need.

Stephanie had taken the train to her apartment outside Paris and would drive back in her own car. Now Carter sat in the rear of the Mercedes, waiting.

"Nick . . ."

He looked up. She was just sliding from a little white Fiat about a half block up on the opposite side of the street.

"Check it one more time," Carter growled.

LeMoine flipped the dash receiver on. At once the car was filled with the hollow beeps being transferred from the envelope in Carter's jacket pocket. The envelope itself had been constructed of a special heavy paper. Through it, five wires thinner than human hairs had been hidden. The wires acted as conductors for a send unit strapped around Carter's middle. Impulses would be sent from Carter and boosted through the envelope to the receiver in the Mercedes. The minicomputer in the car would constantly calibrate the direction in which the envelope was moving and its distance from Carter or the Mercedes.

"You know the gig," Carter said, stepping from the car.

"Got it."

Stephanie crossed the street like a deer and, in moments, joined him. She went to the tips of her toes and brushed his lips with hers.

"Hello. Aren't you going to say anything?"

"Of course. You look marvelous."

She wore a tan trench coat, and a black knitted beret tipped jauntily over one eye. The coat was partially open, revealing a yellow wool sweater that hugged the heavy roundness of her breasts. The skirt was red vinyl and barely came to mid-thigh. She wore black stockings and black, ankle-high boots.

"You said the café is a little punkish."

"It is," Carter said, nodding. He had worn a tweed jacket with patches on the elbows and a dark turtleneck.

"Is something wrong?" Stephanie asked, whisking the hair from her face with a swing of her head.

"Having second thoughts, perhaps. You're sure you want to do this?"

"Of course. It will be fun. I have always had a love of intrigue, even though you won't tell me what it is all about. Shall we go?"

She took his arm and they walked to the corner.

"There it is."

In the middle of the block they saw a blinking neon sign on a three-story building: Café Marie. The small building housing the club seemed squeezed between its two neighbors.

There was a single large door. Carter opened it and they went inside. They were immediately assailed by loud rock music.

Wooden booths covered two walls. The other two were taken up with an elevated bandstand and a bar. On the bandstand were four female frights with purple and green hair. They banged guitars and drums, and were dressed in what appeared to be colorful underwear.

"Punk," Carter said.

"What?" Stephanie asked, leaning her ear to his lips to hear.

"I didn't think it would be quite this awful," he said and chuckled.

She laughed. "Don't worry, Nick—it's all in fun."

There were groups of small tables clustered around the bandstand and a small dance floor. A young girl who could have doubled as one of the band members led them to one of these tables.

Carter requested a booth or a table in the larger room on the second floor, but he was told there were none available.

They sat and ordered drinks.

The noise was deafening. It reverberated around the room and seemed to come up through the floorboards, through Carter's feet, to invade his body.

A few people were packed into a thick mass on the

dance floor. They moved as one creature. He said so, and Stephanie laughed and shrugged, conveying by gesture that she couldn't hear a thing he said.

They made their way through two drinks. Between them, Carter slipped the oilskin-wrapped envelope into her bag.

As the Killmaster ordered a third round, the band took a break. Between the time they left the bandstand and the recorded music started, Carter was able to make himself heard.

"You know what to do?"

She nodded, and he could detect only the slightest bit of hesitancy in her voice when she spoke. "Upstairs john, last stall against the window."

"And?"

"Slide it flat down the back of the tank so it doesn't interfere with the mechanism, and make sure it's submerged."

"Good girl. Go!"

She stood, and Carter watched her mount the stairs and disappear. He leaned back and lit a cigarette.

The band had returned and the dance floor was once again filled with writhing, agonized bodies. Several, he noticed thankfully, were dressed normally. In his tweed jacket, he'd felt very out of place.

Leisurely, he tried to take in most of the women. None paid him any more than glancing attention.

In about ten minutes she was back, leaning across the table to speak into his ear.

"Sorry it took so long. The place was jammed. I had to restore my makeup, comb my hair, and practically redo my nails to get to that booth."

"No problem. Is it done?"

"It's done."

Carter reached beneath his jacket and flipped the

"send" button. At once there was a single pulsing throb against his chest, telling him that he had clicked in with LeMoine and the send/receive unit in the Mercedes.

"Do you dance?" he asked.

"Of course," she said, nodding.

"I don't, to this. But it won't make any difference."

It didn't. All they had to do was join the mass and move in the same general direction. The music was still ear-shattering, but thankfully the tempo had slowed.

Stephanie moved into his arms and buried her face in his neck. With the dance floor so crowded, it wasn't so much dancing as shuffling and swaying.

Carter didn't mind. Stephanie had molded her body to his and he was loving the touch and the smell of her.

"When you do whatever you have to do, will you come back to the hotel?"

"Yes."

"I'll be there."

"That's why I gave you the key to the suite," he whispered in her ear.

It was nearly midnight before the steady throb began against his chest. The envelope had been lifted from the water and activated.

"It's a go," he whispered.

She was good. She hadn't forgotten a single thing Carter had told her. Without a word, she stood and went up the stairs.

Carter let his eyes roam constantly from the stairs to the front door and back again.

It was nearly impossible to tell. The front door kept opening and closing, expelling people as fast as others entered. Far over half of those coming and going were women.

"I found it," she said, slipping back into her chair.

"The oilskin?"

She nodded. "Still wet, wadded up in the wastepaper basket."

The throb was getting weaker against his chest. He threw a handful of bills on the table and grabbed Stephanie's hand.

Outside, they turned right, made the corner, and turned right again. The Mercedes was gone. Carter guided her past the corner where it had been and headed for the Fiat. At the same time, he shook the miniature walkie-talkie from his right sleeve into his palm and brought it to his lips.

"Charley?"

"Yo."

"Did you make her?"

"No, but I've got her beep. From the speed, I'd say she's walking. On the grid it's Saint-Michel toward the river. No . . . wait." There was silence for a few seconds, and then he was back. "She's turned right on Saint-Germain."

"How far are you away from her?"

"Several blocks, no sighting."

"Stay that way," Carter rasped. "Don't let her spot you. I'd say she's good."

"Will do."

They reached the Fiat. "Keys," Carter said.

She handed them over and they both got in. Carter gunned the little engine and they were away.

"One thing," Stephanie said.

"Yeah?"

"You're not a Communist, are you?"

"No," he laughed. "Actually, truthfully, I'm a private detective. And you know what?"

"What?"

"You get part of the fee for this night's work."

Out of the corner of his eye he saw her relax in the passenger seat.

God, he thought, *you get to be such a damned good liar in this business.*

It was a merry chase. The lady walked, cabbed, walked, and cabbed again. The last cab dumped her in Montmartre. There she started walking again, but not for long. LeMoine guessed it was a motor scooter.

Carter sped up, then made a few quick turns in order to pass her in front.

"I've got her! Half blond and half purple hair with a scarf over it. Black leather blouse and miniskirt. She's on a Vespa, and just turned into Rue du Faubourg by Saint-Eugène."

Thirty seconds later, LeMoine came on again. "Got her. She stopped and locked up the Vespa in the parking lot beside Saint-Eugène. She's just tossed something . . . Christ, Nick, it's the envelope! She tossed it into a trash can!"

"Which way?"

"Left on Rue d'Enghien. I've got to go past, Nick. She'll spot me for sure."

Carter gunned the Fiat around two taxis and hung a right on Saint-Denis. At the corner of Rue d'Enghien, he slid to a stop and piled out.

"Stay here!" he barked to Stephanie.

Quickly he ran to the corner, cursing himself for not taking the SDECE boys up on their offer of a backup. His thinking had been that too many cooks would cause their quarry to smell the cookfire.

He had taken the chance, and now might be sorry.

Cautiously he peered around the corner, just in time to see the woman.

It was a drop.

He edged up the street and watched her through the window. The café was crowded, jammed in fact. She could already have passed the message ten times.

Now he would have to stay with her.

Even as he thought this, he saw her rise and head for the door. In her hand she carried a sack.

Maybe not, Carter thought. Maybe she just bought some dinner.

She walked directly across the street and into a hotel. Carter checked the sign: Hotel Oriental. It was old, an eight-floor relic from the past.

Carter edged down the street and into an alley that ran adjacent to the hotel. About fifty yards in, he found it: a side exit.

Quickly he ran back to the car.

"Need one more favor. Here's the scam. You were in that café across the street. You were talking to this girl . . . describe her to the desk clerk. She told you to come up for a drink, but you don't remember her room number and she didn't tell you her name."

"Isn't that a little farfetched?"

Carter smiled. "Of course it is. But when you slip all these bills to the desk clerk, he'll think it's perfectly normal."

Stephanie shrugged and slipped the money into her purse. "This gets crazier all the time. Hey—what are you doing?"

"Trying to make your hair a little wilder. Get out your makeup . . ."

Stephanie followed Carter's instructions about teasing her hair and applying an extra layer of makeup.

"Not bad. With your clothes, you'll pass. Let's hope the guy inside just figures birds of a feather flock together."

Stephanie was shaking her head. "This is crazy."

"*Chérie*, in this business, crazy things usually work just because they're crazy. No, don't put the hat back on."

"What happens after I get the room number?"

"There's an alley exit off the rear of the lobby. Take the stairs up until you're sure the desk clerk has lost interest. Then take the back stairs down and come out that way. I'll be waiting."

He leaned over and pecked her on the cheek as he reached across her body and opened the door.

Stephanie arched an eyebrow. "Just what are you after this woman for?"

Carter thought fast. "She's blackmailing her ex-lover, a married American millionaire. Go!"

She slid from the car, mumbling something like, "In France the wife would say so what, and the mistress would just find another millionaire!"

Carter tracked her with the Fiat until she entered the hotel, then he pulled into the alley. He stopped at the exit door, left the motor running, and stepped from the car.

It was only ten minutes but seemed an eternity. The instant the door cracked, Carter was there to grab it in case she forgot and let it slam shut.

"Well?"

"I don't believe it," she replied.

"What?"

"He believed me and I didn't even give him the money!"

"Which room?"

"Four-eleven, in the rear."

"You're a princess," he said, kissing her and giving her a gentle shove toward the Fiat.

"Nick . . ."

"Yeah?"

"He did say something about crazy foreigners taking over the hotel."

"I'll remember it."

He watched until her taillights disappeared around the corner, and then he slipped into the lobby.

"Mademoiselle," Carter growled, rapping on the door of 411. *"Mademoiselle?"*

"Oui?" The voice came from deep in the room.

He rapped again as if he hadn't heard her. *"Mademoiselle?"*

"Oui?" Nearer now. "What is it?"

"I am staying in the room below yours. Is your tub overflowing?"

"What?"

"Your tub. It must be overflowing. My poor wife is trying to dry her hair in the bathroom, and water from your tub is coming through the ceiling . . ."

The chain started to rattle halfway through Carter's speech. Then he heard the lock click and kept on talking.

"Monsieur, I assure you—"

Carter's shoulder hit the door and the door hit her. She spun backward over a chair and hit the floor on her back. But she was down only an instant.

She was on her feet like a cat and diving for the bed and her purse. Carter lunged at the same time. She saw it and, in midair, twisted.

Both of her knees caught him dead center in the chest. She recovered immediately and made the bed.

The Killmaster saw the silenced, six-inch tube gun in her hand and rolled just in time to avoid the slug. The sound it made firing was no more than a sudden rush of air.

He heard the slug drive into a far wall, and rolled over her. The tube gun was a single shot, so he had no more to fear from it.

Not so the woman.

She was like an octopus, a whirling dervish, with all four of her appendages and her head deadly.

Carter took a couple of good belts in the neck and one in the belly before he could curl his fingers around her neck and press hard with his thumbs just behind her ears.

Even out cold she struggled for a few seconds.

Beneath her skirt she wore black tights. Carter flipped the shoes from her feet, pulled off the tights, and ripped them in half. Then he dragged her into the bathroom and tied one of her wrists securely to the shower rod with one leg of the tights, and the other wrist to the shower head with the other.

Then he went through the hotel room like a dose of salts.

He pulled every dresser drawer, searched what they contained, and checked for anything taped beneath them. He emptied her suitcase and went through it. The far-out garb she wore was evidently the only outfit of its kind she owned. The clothes in the suitcase were fairly conventional and cheap. The few that had labels confirmed that the lady did a lot of traveling—one hell of a lot.

He stripped the bed and looked under the mattress. Nothing. The closet was empty.

He checked the baseboards and behind the furniture. In an ashtray on the bedside stand there was ash residue from a recently burned piece of paper.

Quickly he turned her purse over and dumped its contents on the bed. A fat pen came apart and four spare .45 slugs for the tube gun fell into his hand. Concealed in the handle of her hairbrush was a four-inch stiletto. The powder in her compact had an odd aroma.

He held it far enough from his nose so none of it would go up his nostrils, and tried to nail it.

Eventually it came to him. He nailed the scent just about the same time he spotted the tiny silver fragments of phenol mixed in with the face powder.

It was phenol in its crystalline form, fairly harmless as is. But mixed with water and thrown in someone's face, it becomes a deadly weapon otherwise known as carbolic acid.

Nice lady I've dug up, Carter mused, lifting the passport from a small handful of francs. The passport was Italian.

The date of birth made her twenty-four years old. Probably about right. The place of birth was listed as Genoa, and the name was Lucera Babolini.

Carter was willing to bet the name and place of birth was as phony as the passport. As he slipped it into the false pocket behind his own wallet, there was a light groan and gasp from the bathroom.

Quickly he threw the contents of the purse and all her clothing into the suitcase. He even stripped the pillows and put the cases into the bag. The quilt and two sheets he left on the bed.

As a last thought before closing the bag, he grabbed the compact and slipped it into the false pocket along with her passport.

Using his own razor-sharp stiletto, Hugo, he cut about five feet out of the middle of the phone cord and stripped it. He cut a one-inch gash in the television power line and wrapped one bare end of the telephone cord securely to the bare TV wire.

He then unplugged the television and carted it into the bathroom.

The woman was stirring but was not fully awake. Carter set the television on the floor and filled the water pitcher from the cold tap.

Unceremoniously, he threw the water into her face.

She came to, blubbering and cursing. Carter could curse—and understand cursing—in fifteen languages, including Arabic and Farsi.

"Your passport is Italian. Where are you really from?"

She glowered.

"What's your real name?"

She spat at him, barely missing his face. He flat-handed her left cheek and backhanded the right.

"Did you already deliver the message from Allad Khopar?"

"What do you know of Khopar?" she gasped reflexively. Her English was almost fluent.

Carter smiled. "How do you think I found you?"

"American?"

"Yes."

"Pig." She spat again.

Carter ignored it. "I don't have a great deal of time to waste on you. I want the Puppet Master. I know he's in Paris. Where?"

"Fuck you."

Carter sent Hugo's gleaming edge toward her right wrist, the one attached to the shower head. She tensed but didn't cry out.

Instead of cutting her, he cut the nylon fabric, freeing her right arm. "Take off your clothes."

"What?"

"Remove your clothes."

"Kiss my ass."

"Some other time." He gathered the front of her blouse in his right hand. Pushing her chest above her breasts with his left, he shredded the garment from her body.

"Son of a pig!" she wheezed in Arabic.

"The rest . . . down to skin."

She tried to kick him. It was futile. Carter chopped her ankle and she screamed in pain.

He reached for her bra. She slithered away, fumbling with the clasp between her breasts. The wispy garment came off and she threw it in his face.

He waited a few seconds and she struggled from the skirt. She kicked it away and stood in the sheer black panties she wore under the tights.

"Those, too."

She curled her thumb in the panties and pushed them down until she could also kick them in his direction. She stood nakedly defiant in front of him, her perfect body as taut as a string.

"Is it rape you want?" she hissed.

"It's the Puppet Master, Amin Koulami, I want. Where is he?"

Silence, her black eyes unwavering, her full breasts rising and falling with the anger in each breath she took.

"One last time. Where is Koulami?"

She turned her face from him.

Carter grabbed her right wrist and retied it, this time to the lower faucet. He turned on the shower, full force on cold, and plugged in the television set.

The way she was tied, she could not rise at all and she could only move a few inches forward or backward. In short, she couldn't get out of the water that had risen above her ankles.

When he draped the bare end of the television wire over the edge of the tub, she gasped in realization.

"My God, you are going to electrocute me . . ."

"Only in stages," he replied.

"You can't torture me," she hissed, a red flush over-powering the olive tone of her face. "I have been tor-tured by experts . . . the SAVAK."

Carter dropped the bare end of the wire into the water for a millisecond, and yanked it right back out.

Her chest tried to scream but her throat was too con-stricted. Her back arched and every muscle and tendon in her stood out in definition.

"Where is Amin Koulami?"

The defiance in her black eyes bordered on being spectacular. He had never seen such a degree of defiance and hatred in one face.

The Killmaster wasn't kidding himself. This one was a fanatic, and a woman. Women naturally had more tolerance for pain in their minds and bodies than most men. It came with being a woman and having the knowledge that one day she might have to endure the ultimate pain, childbirth.

And this woman, whoever she was, could probably stand more pain than her sisters.

No, Carter wasn't kidding himself. He was merely playing a game . . . with only a fifty-fifty chance of win-ning.

"Where is Koulami?"

He didn't wait for an answer. He knew there was none coming.

This time he left the bare wire in the water three times as long.

Again the body became like a board. She managed to emit one strangled scream that was drowned by the shower and the TV before she passed out.

Carter went into the other room and lit a cigarette at the window.

They were on high ground, and the buildings across the street were low.

Even from the fourth floor, he was looking out at the sparkling lights of Paris flowing in an unbroken line to the Seine and beyond to the Left Bank and the countryside.

"Nice postcard," he murmured, and shook the mike into his palm. "Charley."

"Here. Christ, where the hell are you? I've got a fix on you from your belt beeper, but I can't nail it without leaving the car."

"I'm in a room on the fourth floor of the Hotel Oriental. I can see you parked across the street about half a block away."

"The girl?"

"If you mean Stephanie, she's back at the Ritz, I hope." Then he went on to explain the situation. "No guarantee, but if this one comes out, be ready to pick me up."

"Right on. What about the locals?"

"Just the SDECE people, and keep them in backup."

"Will do. Be careful."

"Yeah." Carter slipped the mike back up his sleeve and returned to the bathroom.

The woman was awake and glaring, but she was worn down. There was fear in her eyes now as Carter bent to retrieve the wire.

But he also saw cunning.

"Where is Koulami?"

"Go to hell." He started playing out the wire. "No, my God, not again . . ."

"Where . . ."

"Please, I beg you, please . . ."

"Where is Koulami!"

"Fifteen Rue Legendre, flat Four-C. Please . . ."

"How many with him?"

"Two . . . bodyguards."

"What's the address again?"

"Fifteen Rue Legendre. It is near Saint-Marie."

Carter unplugged the television and gathered her clothes from the floor. He showed her the mike.

"If Koulami is not there, I have a man nearby who will come up here and plug the television back in."

The fear on her face as he turned away was almost real.

He stuffed the shredded clothes into the bag, snapped it, and left the room. The elevator indicator above the door pointed to "L." He hoped it stayed there. This time of night it probably would.

The bag went down the garbage shoot. Carter went into the maid's linen closet. He cracked the door a fraction of an inch, secured it, and sat down to wait.

FOUR

The headlights picked out the potholes in the narrow, hard-packed dirt road, but there were far too many of them for the driver of the old Land-Rover to avoid. For every two potholes they avoided, the wheels would drop in one with a bone-jarring thud.

There were three dark-clad figures in the Land-Rover, two in front and one in the rear. Beside the rear-seat passenger, AK-47 assault rifles, bars of C-4 plastique explosive, fragmentation grenades, and extra magazines were neatly arranged.

A Saab truck followed the Land-Rover. It was driven by a dour-faced giant whose head was wreathed in smoke from the hashish cigarette between his lips.

"How much further?" asked the driver of the Land-Rover.

"Four kilometers to the village," replied the man in the rear, playing a penlight over the map on his lap. "Another three to the plant."

The driver nodded. "Right on schedule."

They rode in silence the rest of the way to the village

of Trapur. There they slowed, unwilling to chance killing one of India's sacred animals. None of the men wanted to draw any attention to the passing of their vehicles through the village.

Ten minutes later they pulled off onto yet a smaller road. A half mile farther on, they stopped and killed the lights.

As one, the three men gathered their weapons and moved from the Land-Rover to the crest of the hill beside the road.

Nestled at the bottom of the gorge, about a quarter of a mile below them, was the Trapur nuclear power plant. It was lit from every conceivable angle. Searchlights on automat rotors scanned the chain link fence surrounding it. A ring of lights ran around the roof of every building, and more lights gleamed from the few windows.

"Achmed!"

"Yes?" replied the truckdriver from the darkness behind them.

"Remember, do not go until you see the flare." The speaker was a small man with dark, almost delicate, features. Although his voice carried great authority, his appearance was that of a young boy.

In fact he was just twenty-one years old. His name was Shakib.

He was Amin Koulami's younger brother.

"I remember."

The three men checked their watches, nodded, and started down the dusty, rock-strewn hill. Halfway to the bottom they detoured away from the lights. By the time they had reached the bottom they were in the only shadowed place around the plant: directly behind the huge reactor cone.

Without a word, the fence was cut and all three men rolled through silently. Each ran in a different direction.

One minute later all communication between the plant and the rest of India—both telephone and computer—had been severed.

There were two walking guards around the reactor cone. Both of these men were silently killed with garrotes of spring-loaded piano wire.

This done, the three men converged again and ran silently across the lighted compound toward the watch commander's shed. It was located beside the rear entrance to the main plant.

Their timing was perfect. Three minutes after they had settled into the shadows between the shed and the whitewashed main building, the electronically operated door opened.

The watch commander, a uniformed officer in the Indian army, stepped out carrying a tray. On the tray was a teapot and three cups.

The officer and his two subordinates had tea every night at the same time.

Shakib Koulami raised a Soviet-made 9mm Stechkin pistol in both hands. He fired twice. The slugs entered the front of the man's skull one inch apart.

He had barely hit the ground when one man was at the door holding it and the other had retrieved the officer's keys.

He unlocked the shed and within seconds had turned off the plant's interior alarm system.

The interior door, to the plant proper, could only be opened by dialing the correct code into its electronic lock.

They didn't have those codes. Shakib burst by his comrade who was already blocking the outer door open.

He pressed an eighth of a cube of C-4 into the cracks around both hinges and jammed a detonator into each glob.

Ten seconds later, with all three men flattened against the outside wall, the blast tore the hinges loose. Their combined strength pushed it open enough for them to squeeze through.

At this time of night there were only three engineers on duty inside the plant. One of them was in a room just off the tunnel leading to the reactor. His job was to watch the various gauges that read out the amount of heat controlled by the constant cooling system.

A second man was in the master control room, monitoring the amount of power being put out and where it was directed in the Bombay region.

The third man handled the phone and computer system that directed the outstations to cut back or increase power through their feeder lines to various parts of the country according to need.

At that moment, this man was cursing the system's failure and dialing codes that would activate the backup system.

He couldn't get the backup system to work either.

This was an emergency situation. He tried to raise the power control room and request a cutback until he could determine the reason for the failure of his computers and phones.

The intraplant phone system was also out. He would have to go below and order the cutback in person.

Cursing the fact that this happened on his watch, he dialed his code into the door lock and stepped into the hall.

He never saw the man that killed him.

Both of the other engineers were intent on their

various gauges when the waddings of C-4 blew open the doors behind them.

Both of them died without turning around in their chairs.

It was well rehearsed, clockwork perfection. Seventeen minutes after rolling through the fence, the three men were packing the door of the main storage room that contained lead-lined casks of nuclear reactor fuel.

At the same time, the man named Achmed was charging down the road toward the plant's main gate. The gate was time-controlled, set to open twice a day for the changing shifts. There was an outer and inner fence, with a parking area between. The gate on the inner fence was also time-controlled.

The front of the truck Achmed drove had two special characteristics that had been added to its factory construction.

The enclosed box behind its cab was lead-lined and self-contained. By throwing two levers, the box could be detached from the truck bed. On its bottom, small wheels similar to those beneath the legs of a piano had been attached. Because of these wheels, the box could be moved anywhere over a smooth surface by only one man.

The second alteration in the truck was its nose. The entire front end had been bolstered and reinforced with steel bars and plates. It had been made into a formidable battering ram.

Achmed splintered the first gate and rolled on through the second. In the inner compound he turned left and, hardly slacking his speed, raced for the loading dock outside the storage room.

The door was already sliding up as Achmed backed the truck up to the lip of the dock. They met perfectly.

The truck had scarcely rocked to a halt when two men darted forward. They flipped the levers, and with a gentle push the box rolled from the truck bed, across the loading dock, and into the storage area.

Shakib Koulami awaited it. He had already selected the four lead-lined casks of nuclear reactor fuel that were to be stolen.

"Hurry!" he hissed, consulting his watch. "We have only four minutes and twenty seconds to stay on schedule!"

In the distance, the four men could hear the steady drone of a helicopter.

In the rear of the canteen on the plant's first floor was a small storage room. Besides the supplies for the canteen, the room contained a cot that was often used by workers to catch a quick nap between the rush of meals.

On this night the cot was occupied by a drowsing Pal Ramaj. Earlier, Ramaj had dawdled too long while cleaning one of the offices. By the time he had finished and put his equipment away, he had missed the last bus to Trapur.

It happened rarely, but when it did, the night engineers always allowed him to use the cot rather than walk home to the village. It was good for them, actually. They didn't have to make their own tea and midwatch food.

The sound of Achmed's truck crashing through the gate brought Ramaj to his feet. He thought, in his dreaming, that he had heard gunfire and explosives. But to those he had paid little attention. They were part of his dream. Ramaj often thought of war in his dreams. He wanted to be a soldier.

But the roar of the truck crashing through the gates was another matter.

He bolted through the canteen area and up the stairs to the second floor. He saw the body from the landing, and then heard the roar of the helicopter.

Instantly he was down the length of the opposite hall and staring out at the parking lot.

A helicopter was landing. He saw movement below to his right. A truck was pulling away from the loading dock. He could see four men, all in black, with guns slung over their shoulders.

Ramaj was not a highly educated man. But he had survived in India for twenty-two years by being observant and cunning.

Without a second thought he ran back down to the main floor. Down a long hallway and then down a second flight of stairs, he came to the door of the armory. He already had his keys in his hands.

Inside, he pried the leg from one of the workbenches and went to work on the lock of the main arms cabinet. Like a wild man he pounded until the lock sprung and the door swung open.

He knew exactly what he was doing. He had spent hours down here with the soldiers. They all liked him and enjoyed showing off by explaining the way each gun worked.

He hoisted a .303 Vickers Berthier machine gun with tripod legs to his shoulder. He jammed a thirty-round magazine into the feed and filled his pocket with four more.

Back in the hall, he ran for the elevator that would take him up to the roof and the observation deck.

• • •

Rami Sherif handled the big Bell like the expert she was. She settled gently onto the parking lot, feathered the rotors, and ran to the rear cargo door.

She had barely slid it open before the box was being rolled in.

Shakib Koulami stood by the door of the truck grinning at her. "Any trouble?"

"None."

"I didn't think there would be. He couldn't resist you."

"Clear!" Achmed cried.

"Batten it down," Shakib ordered, climbing into the cab of the truck. "Rami, get ready to fly!"

She threw her head back with an exhilarated laugh and darted back to the cockpit. Seconds later, Achmed was at her shoulder.

"The box is secure."

They both watched the truck. Shakib parked it and dropped from the cab. He ran toward the helicopter with his AK above his head, shaking it in the victory sign.

Rami could see his perfect white teeth gleaming in a smile.

And then she saw the mouth drop open and blood spew. His eyes widened with shock and his body lifted into the air as if he had been swatted by a giant hand.

"Shakib!" she screamed when the body turned in the air and she saw the bloody rents in the back of his shirt.

"There, on the roof!" Achmed shouted, pointing.

She looked and saw the orange bursts. Shakib's body was being riddled where it lay on the asphalt.

There was a momentary lull while the shooter changed magazines. Then the orange bursts started again. She saw the spurts in the asphalt where the bullets hit.

The shooter was finding the range of the helicopter.

The two in the rear of the machine were firing back. This was throwing off the aim of the man on the roof, but it wouldn't for long.

"Fly!" Achmed shouted.

"But Shakib . . ."

"Fly! It's too late for Shakib now!"

Rami Sherif pushed forward on the throttle. They lifted.

At the same time she whirled, giving the man on the roof the smaller target of the helicopter's tail.

"Hurry!" Achmed shouted over the ear-shattering noise.

"I am!" she replied. "It's the weight!"

She gave the machine full power. The nose tilted, and at last they began to move.

In seconds they were zigzagging out of range.

"How?" she cried. "How? It was the perfect plan!"

"A miscalculation," Achmed replied with a shrug, and lit a hashish cigarette.

FIVE

It took over a half hour, about ten minutes longer than Carter expected, for the woman to free herself.

He stiffened and leaned forward, putting his eye as close as possible to the crack in the linen closet door. Then her door opened. She looked both ways in the hall and then darted to the elevator.

As it clanged up from the lobby, Carter took in her far-less-than-designer gown and smiled.

The lady was a thinker, and a creative one at that.

She had taken the bed sheet and draped it around her like an Indian sari. It was held in place by some clever tucks and folds, and was sashed at the waist with a slice of cord from the venetian blinds.

She might draw a few stares on the street, but probably more for her bare feet than the unusual dress.

The elevator door closed behind her and the Killmaster burst from his place of concealment.

"I'll be damned," he hissed as he took one look at the moving indicator and ran for the stairs.

The indicator, which he had expected to be heading

back down to the lobby, was going the other way.

And then he remembered the desk clerk's words to Stephanie about crazy foreigners taking over the hotel.

Koulami had probably moved in bag, baggage, and entourage, and made the place a base of operations.

Carter was running about even, maybe a second or two behind the elevator on floors five and six. At each landing he paused to make sure the old cage was still grinding. When it was, he continued climbing.

When he was sure there was no stop on seven, he increased his speed and shook down the mike.

"Charley!"

"Yeah?"

"He's here."

"In the hotel?"

"Yeah. Somewhere on the eighth floor . . . I think . . . I hope. Have you got backup?"

"Yeah. They've agreed to play backup unless you give the word."

That meant only one thing. The French feds wanted Koulami out of the way as much as AXE did, and they were only too happy to let Carter do the job. That left them with only garbage cleanup and paper work.

"I'll try and find out what the big score is before I terminate," Carter growled into the mike.

"Keep me posted."

"As soon as I know."

Carter released the talk button and let the spring-cord pull the mike back up his sleeve. He filled his hand with Wilhelmina and crouched in the shadows of the eighth-floor landing.

His luck was too good to be believed.

The landing where he crouched was about ten feet starboard of the elevator. The door the woman went to was directly across the hall and halfway between the elevator and the landing.

He would be able to hit them before they had an inkling of warning.

She rapped sharply and there was an instant reply from beyond the door.

"It is me, Anis."

So much for Lucera Babolini, Carter thought, flipping the safety off the Luger and dropping into a tenser crouch.

The door cracked open and she started to slide through.

Carter moved, doing everything in one fluid motion. He cracked the door with his shoulder, curled his left arm around the woman's shoulder and neck, and charged into the room with the Luger arcing.

There were three of them, all short, dark, and Middle Eastern-looking. The door had barely slammed shut before three ugly little Walther PPKs had popped into their hands.

"Anis, you stupid bitch. You've led them right to us!"

"No, I sent him—"

"Shut up!"

It was the one in the middle speaking. Besides his voice, everything about him bespoke authority. Carter focused on him.

"Amin Koulami, I assume."

"I know no Koulami. Who are you?"

All three of them started to move as one.

"Don't do it," Carter hissed, tipping the silencer up until the business end was ground under the chin of Anis/Lucera. "Stalemate."

Koulami had managed a couple of feet further than

his comrades. He stood flatfooted, the Walther steady
in both hands, waist high, taking in Carter and the
woman.

"Amin, I am sorry . . ."

"Shut up, you stupid whore. What do you want?" he
snarled to Carter.

The Killmaster watched them all carefully for a moment, but he was able to take in the rest of the room as
well.

It had truly been set up as a base of operations. All
the furniture had been pushed to the walls. In its place
an elaborate radio setup had been spread out. Carter
could tell from the equipment that it had a lot of range.
Charts were on the walls and a portable computer rested
on a coffee table.

"To start with, I want those charts, the pages I see by
the radio, and the software from the computer."

"Your French is good, but I think that you are not
French. American?"

"Get the material," Carter barked, grinding a little
harder with the gun.

Koulami's hard black eyes shifted from Carter to the
woman momentarily, and then he turned. He gathered
the material, except for the charts, and started back.

It was in his eyes. Carter could see it, sense it from the
way he was bringing the Walther back up.

But still the Killmaster didn't believe it until it was too
late.

From five feet away, Koulami began firing point-
blank into the woman's body. She shook in Carter's
hands. He felt one of the slugs rip through and slam into
his left side.

He tried to right Wilhelmina and fire, but he got off
only one wild one before the other two goons were on

him. They pummeled him with their Walthers on the head, neck, and shoulders. He felt the woman being wrenched from his grasp, and then a wrist chop made him drop the Luger.

He was going down and everything behind his eyeballs was alternating black and red. His knees hit the floor and the carpet came up to meet him.

He was fading, but he could hear Koulami giving orders.

"Gather up . . . we can carry . . . we will have to leave the equipment . . . no, don't shoot him . . . there are other ways . . ."

And then Carter passed out.

He was familiar with the nausea and the aching muscles when he awakened. He opened his eyes, but they wouldn't focus. There were fuzzy faces that wouldn't remain in one place.

"He's awake."

"Roll up his sleeve!"

He felt the needle go into his arm, and almost immediately the ache and the nausea went away. It was replaced by a feeling of euphoria.

He was fading, but he could hear the crackling of a radio . . . and a voice . . . and then Koulami's voice replying.

"It is sad, but he is one with Allah now . . . we have learned of Brussman's whereabouts . . . meet us in three days' time at . . ."

Someone poured a bottle of ink over Carter's eyes and it seeped clear through to his brain.

He was even foggier when he came around again. He opened one eye and then the other. He couldn't make anything move, but he could see, albeit with very fuzzy vision.

He was in a car. It was still night, moonlight. There were trees running swiftly by the windows. Countryside.

Whatever drug they had given him was wearing off slowly.

He came alert enough to realize he was in the back of a taxi. There was a partition between the front and back seat. He could see the driver, one of Koulami's boys, leering at him in the rearview mirror.

He looked around. Anis/Lucera's bullet-ridden body lolled in the seat beside him. His own Luger was in his lap. A Walther was in the seat between them.

And then he noticed his door: no handle.

He concentrated, moving one arm and then the other. Eventually he was able to sit up. He leaned forward, put his head between his knees, and gulped several deep breaths.

The exertion made him woozy and created a burning pain in his left side. Gingerly he pulled his coat aside. His shirt was half gone, and around what was left there was a huge clot of blood.

Then he remembered. One of the Walther's slugs had gone right through the woman and caught him.

Gently, he examined the wound. It was only a gash. Her body had taken most of the punch and Wilhelmina's holster had absorbed the rest.

The Luger was empty. He holstered it and checked the Walther. It was the same.

The driver was still leering as he slowed the car. Carter searched and saw only wilderness, plowed fields, trees, a dirt road.

The driver got out, opened the hood, and worked for a few seconds beneath it. Then, giving Carter a last hideous grin around the side of the hood, he turned and started walking. Soon he was jogging.

Then, as realization of what was going to happen hit Carter, the driver was running just as fast as his legs would carry him.

Carter tried to galvanize himself into action, and immediately felt sicker. He lurched across the woman's body and tried the opposite door handle. It, too, was gone.

He pounded on the glass partition with his fists.

The nausea got worse.

He lay on the seat and tried to kick the side glass out with his feet. It didn't budge; it wouldn't even crack.

Then he did get sick.

It made the ache come back into his muscles. They slowed and his mind began to join them.

Hang on, he screamed at himself, *you can't pass out!*

Wildly he looked around the car for something stronger than his weakened legs to use on the windows.

Nothing.

He pushed the woman to the floorboard and yanked out the bottom of the seat. There was just a chance that he could get something from the trunk, a jack handle perhaps, if he could get into the trunk. Feverishly, his hands shaking, he worked at the screws holding the seat back.

It came loose and he pushed it aside. Behind it he found solid steel.

Everything was becoming fuzzy and seen through tunnel vision. He knew what was going to happen. He knew the car was going to blow. The question was, how soon?

He went back to the glass partition and pounded on it until, even through the numbness caused by the dope, he could feel pain in his hands.

He retched again.

Between his pounding and clawing, a slice of the wooden panel between the glass and the seat back came loose. He worked at that, more out of anger and frustration than any sense of purpose, until he had it mangled and ripped away.

And then a purpose entered his befogged brain. He could see down into the hollow back of the front seat. Using his penknife and his fingernails, he ripped and hacked at the upholstery until he had a hole in the base behind it. Then he lurched back and pounded at it with his feet.

"Kick, kick, kick!" he screamed aloud at his weakening legs.

At last the hole was big enough. He fell forward, throwing his hands into the hole. He searched for and found the wiring. He didn't have time or the eyesight to figure out which went to the windows, which to seats, which to cigarette lighter, lights, or the myriad other electrical accouterments of the car. He just took Hugo and started sawing.

At last he was through them all. He put the stiletto in his teeth and rotated bare ends to bare ends. There was a sizzling sound and the scorching stench of flesh.

It was his own. But he didn't stop, and at last he heard a whirring sound from the bowels of the seat.

He looked up. The glass divider was just disappearing into the seat.

Struggling, his stomach in knots, sure that his muscles had totally atrophied, he managed to pull himself through the opening and fall into the front seat.

He rolled from the driver's side and somehow got to his feet. He lurched into a plowed field and ran. He fell, somehow staggered back to his feet, and ran on.

He'd never make it, no way.

He fell again.

He was crawling when the ground shook beneath him.

An instant later the sound of the blast rolled through the field. He craned his head around in time to see parts of the car hit the earth a football field away. The blast had cut the car clean in half.,

He thought of the woman in the car. So much for Koulami's loyalty to his puppets. And so much for Anis Whoever-the-hell-she-once-was.

He got to his feet and staggered into the trees.

It might have been an hour, it might have been five. Carter didn't know. He had lost all track of time and direction. He had put as much distance between himself and the explosion as possible. Twice he had passed out, and another time he realized he had been going around in a large circle for an hour.

Somehow all the roads he had found led nowhere but back into thick trees.

He was close to delirium when he saw the light. It was about a hundred yards off the dirt road, through more trees.

As he stumbled toward it he realized that it was almost dawn. He could sense the first beginnings of gray light through the canopy of trees above him.

It was a farmhouse, a low, sprawling building of another age, in disrepair and badly in need of a coat of paint.

But there was a light.

Carter got to one of the windows and stared in.

He saw a buxom older woman with frizzy gray hair.

She was wearing old torn slippers, a man's shirt that was too small for her ample bust, and a wrinkled skirt that was strained by her wide hips. She was ironing a shirt, the iron plugged into an outlet near the door.

On the wall behind her head Carter saw a telephone.

He walked down a weed-choked path to the front door. Leaning against the doorframe, he pulled Wilhelmina from the holster and, holding it by the barrel, rapped on the door.

There was no response. As he raised the gun again, the door opened and the woman stood there, the hot end of the iron inches from Carter's face.

"No, please . . . accident . . . have to use your phone . . ."

"*Non!* Go away!"

"Please. Don't want to rob you . . . hurt you. Here . . ."

He held the Luger up butt-first to her. She eyed it and the mess he was.

"Please. I'm a police officer," he lied. "Phone."

She snatched the Luger from his hand and stepped back. Carter took two steps into the room and fell flat on his face.

The next thing he knew there was a cool cloth bathing his face.

"You are shot," she said.

"Yes."

"It was clotted. You will live. I was once a nurse."

"Call for me, Paris four-four-four-nine-ten."

She repeated the number.

"Ask for Charley . . . tell him Carter."

"Carter . . . Charley."

"That's right. Just Charley . . ."

And he passed out again.

SIX

Groggy but game, Carter fought his way out of the blackness. Everything was red, but he managed to get his eyes open and keep them that way. They focused on white, with wrinkles. Then dark hair with patches of gray was added to it.

"Welcome back to the living, Monsieur Carter."

"Who are you?"

"My name is Nesbitt. I am the doctor who put you back together."

Carter rolled his eyes around the sterile room. It was all white and windowless. "Where am I?"

"A private clinic near Versailles."

Carter nodded. He had heard of it, a place where SDECE people and friendlies could go when the roof had fallen in on them. A place where they either got patched up or died quietly out of sight.

"How long have I been here?"

"Since around eight this morning."

"And what time is it now?"

The doctor glanced at his wrist. "Almost six."

"Six P.M.?"

"That's right."

"Jesus."

"I must say you have marvelous recuperative power-ers."

"What ails me?"

The man lifted a chart from the end of the bed and read his casualty report. "You have a minor concussion, a lacerated right ear, a broken nose, two cracked ribs, serious bruises on both shoulders and the upper back, and a gash in your left side that appears to have been made by a large-caliber bullet. Other than that, you're a fine physical specimen."

Carter managed a grin under the bandages. "Any of my people here I can talk to?"

He nodded. "I was told to summon a Monsieur Le-Moine when you showed signs of waking up. He should be here in a few minutes."

"Thanks."

The doctor was gone only a few seconds when a starchy little number in white with short blond hair and a no-nonsense stare glided in and grabbed his wrist.

"Is there anything I can get you?"

"Cigarette, scotch, food, and another cigarette . . . in that order."

Her face managed to crack a smile. "Cigarettes are a no-no. Scotch is out of the question. But I will bring you a tray."

Carter went through juice and an omelet and was down to coffee when a weary, gray-faced Charley Le-Moine arrived.

"How goes it, hot dog?"

"They tell me I'll live. Gimme a cigarette."

LeMoine produced two, lit them, and passed one to

Carter. The Killmaster inhaled deeply, hurt, and coughed.

"Jesus, that tastes good. Lay it on me!"

"He got away," LeMoine sighed.

"He *what?*"

"Koulami slipped us."

"How?"

"I read it like this. One bozo takes you down the back stairs of the hotel."

"With the woman's body."

"Right. By the way, she was one Anis Jarocam, student at the University of Beirut until she helped blow it up. We think she was part of the Shiite raiding team that blew up a busload of Israeli kids on the frontier about a year ago. She also set up the assassination of an Israeli couple in Nice last month. The rest of her record reads like a fanatic's manual."

"Nice lady."

"Yeah," LeMoine growled, opening the brief he had carried in with him. "You can sure pick 'em. Anyway, the bozo drives you and the woman out to the country to go boom. By the way, she had five thirty-eight slugs in her. Know anything about that?"

"In a minute. Tell me about Koulami."

"Bozo number two comes out of the hotel. We're set up, but we don't know who he is and we don't know your situation. He barely hits the sidewalk, spots us, and it's the Fourth of July."

"He opened up?" Carter said.

"With a machine pistol. He had it under his raincoat. The SDECE boys made him about twelve pounds heavier before he went down. Then we took the hotel."

"And no Koulami."

"That's about it. We got his radio and computer

gear, but he was air. He probably went over the roof while we were doing the O.K. corral bit in the street.''

Carter nodded. "It would fit." He told LeMoine about the cold-blooded killing of the woman while he was using her as a shield. By the time he was finished, the other man's face was a shade grayer.

"Jesus, he's one cold son of a bitch. You mean the one in the street did a suicide number so Koulami could disappear?''

"I'd bet on it," Carter said. "That's why they're puppets and he's the puppet master.''

Both men fell silent. Carter snuffed the butt and tried to put his mind in gear. "Do you think he's in Paris?''

"No. I doubt if he's even in the country now. He's smooth, slick, and fast. Also, nobody on our side knows what the hell he looks like. He's hard to pin.''

Carter grunted. "Nobody on our side knows what he looks like but me.''

"Yeah," LeMoine said, "that could be a plus, eventually.''

Then Carter remembered. "What about Stephanie, the stewardess?''

"We cleaned you out of the Ritz. This was on top of your bag.''

Carter took the note and unfolded it:

My job is not as exciting as yours, but it's the only one I have. I have to go do it. I hope you get your blackmailer. If you're still in Paris on my next day off, here's my phone number and address.

The number and address and a big *S* followed.

"We checked," LeMoine said. "She's back on the Paris/Nice/Marseille/Paris daily. Looks like no problem.''

"There won't be. No way they could get a connection, especially with the . . . what was her name?''

"Jarocam.''

"Yeah, with her dead.''

LeMoine took a tiny recorder from his pocket and set it on Carter's chest. "We didn't get crap from any of the hotel rooms, not even a print. Want to put down everything you can remember about what happened and what you heard up there?''

"Sure.''

He tried. He concentrated until his head hurt one hell of a lot worse than before.

But all he could remember were the physical parts, and voices while he was going under.

"Great. What did the voices say?''

More concentration and, if anything, a bigger blank.

"*Nada*. If there was anything big in what they said, it didn't register.''

LeMoine shrugged and packed up the recorder. "Maybe it'll come by morning. I'll dictate a report for you tonight and get it on the wire.''

"Thanks.''

"Get some sleep.''

"Will do,'' Carter said. "Leave your cigarettes.''

LeMoine set matches and cigarettes on the bedside table and strode out.

Five minutes later the blond nurse came in and whisked them into her uniform pocket.

"I told you,'' she said, fanning the air.

"You're a perverse witch.''

"I also have a ninety percent record of discharging live patients. Here, take this.''

"What is it?''

"A sleeping pill.''

He didn't think he needed it, but he took it. "Do me a favor?"

"If I can."

"Send a dozen roses to this person at this address." He scrawled Stephanie's name on the note and handed it to her.

"Roses are out of season."

"Then send a dozen of something . . . very beautiful and very expensive."

"Any card?"

"Yeah. Tell her it was a hell of a flight. We'll do it again some time."

He dozed for about an hour and then she was back.

"You have a call. I told them you were—"

"I'll take it." He waited until she had scowled her way out of the room. "Yeah?"

"Charley, Nick. Hell's apoppin'!"

"How so?"

"Don't know the details, but the wires are humming. They just ID'd Koulami's little brother in Trapur, India. That's a piss in the wind from Bombay. He's dead, with about twenty slugs in him."

"Who iced him?"

"A janitor."

"What?"

"Do you know what's at Trapur, Nick?"

"Not offhand."

"It's a nuclear reactor station. Koulami the younger was ripping off nuclear reactor fuel."

"Jesus."

"Yeah, looks like our boy may be going big time. At least D.C. thinks so. Hawk and Company are taking the night flight out of Dulles. They want you at eight in the morning. I'll have a car pick you up."

"You're on. 'Night."

"One more thing . . ."

"Yeah?"

"A crazy hunch," LeMoine said, "and maybe nothing. But your old subconscious may have something in it you don't know about."

"You mean the conversation in the hotel room?"

"Yeah. I'd like to dig for it."

"How?"

"Don't laugh. I'd like to try you first thing in the morning with a hypnotist."

Carter almost did laugh, and then saw the reasoning behind the other man's thinking.

"Sure, why not?"

"See you then."

Carter hung up, lay back on the pillows, and closed his eyes.

As he dropped off, his body reacted to the thought running through his brain. He could feel the woman in his arms as the slugs from the Walther ripped through her.

Even though heat was circulating through the big car, there was cold in Carter's bones. He pulled the collar of the trench coat up around his neck and wriggled further into it. Outside the car there was a clammy mood to the morning, as if it were about to snow or rain. He glanced over at the young agent who had picked him up just after dawn at the clinic.

His hair was sandy blond, his haircut was as precise as his suit, and his jaw was square and perfectly shaved. Carter suspected that the man had shaved twice that morning.

He was the new breed. Carter felt old and tired even though they had brought him new clothes from the skin out.

Carter lit his sixth cigarette of the morning and leaned back with a sigh. Out of the corner of his eye he saw the younger man's nose twitch.

"You don't smoke."

"No, sir."

"How long have you been in?"

"Two years," he replied, a slight flush creeping up his neck. He knew who the scarred veteran was beside him.

"How long in the field?"

"Six months."

"And you don't smoke?"

"No, sir."

"You will."

They headed away from the Seine and in no time passed all the places Carter thought they might be going. Then they started through the back streets of Pigalle, with its cafés, porno houses, and small nightclubs.

Five minutes later they were climbing the hill behind Sacré-Coeur. The old church, partially shrouded in fog, looked like a wealthy matron after a long, hard night.

They parked in the church parking lot where, in an hour or two, the first tourist buses would pull in to discharge their hordes of people and carbon monoxide on the old matron.

"What the hell are we doing in Montmartre?"

"It's an SDECE safe house, sir, right off the artists' square."

They walked down from the church and out onto the square. It was already, even at this early hour, lined with umbrellas, rickety, makeshift stands, and wobbling tables full of paints and brushes.

Artists milled around in heavy coats, fur-fringed jackets, and faded denim. They drank coffee and blinked sleep from their eyes. From somewhere came the tinny sound of rock and roll, and there was the distinct smell of marijuana in the air.

"Jesus, Renoir would die," Carter murmured.

"Beg your pardon, sir?"

"Nothing. Is this it?"

It was a flat, three-story building off the square, with an ornate door and tightly curtained windows.

The door opened on the first ring, and both men darted inside. A clone of Carter's driver led him down a long hall without a word. He opened a door and Carter entered a woody, low-ceilinged room with books lining every wall.

A fire crackled and a bear of a man with a seamed, kindly face, white fringe around a bald head, and a steaming cup of coffee in his hand warmed his backside against it.

"Carter?"

"Good morning."

"I'm Jeffrey Rudder." Carter shook the proffered hand. "Did they give you any pills this morning?"

Carter shook his head. "I'm supposed to take a couple of antibiotics and a painkiller when you're finished with me."

"Good. Have you ever been hypnotized before?"

"A couple of times. They tell me I'm not a good subject."

The old man slurped his coffee. "It often depends on the circumstances and the surroundings. This isn't the best, but it will have to do. They said you took a pretty bad beating and were shot. That won't help. The trauma might interfere.''

Carter slumped into a chair by the fireplace and chuckled. "Don't worry about that. I lost the ability to be traumatized years ago. Shall we begin?''

They sat at a large round table in a third-floor room. It, too, had a roaring fire. Coffee and croissants were in the middle of the table, and there was the smell of old leather from the furniture in the air.

Charley LeMoine was to Carter's right. A large, square-jawed man with gray eyes and a Mierschaum in his teeth that never stopped billowing smoke was to Carter's left. He was Christian Peterson, head of the International Nuclear Regulatory Commission.

To Peterson's left was François Shelbain, director of the *Service de Documentation Extérieure et de Contre-Espionnage*. For short, SDECE, the French secret service.

Shelbain was about fifty, but his clear, cold blue eyes were thousands of years old. He had seen and done it all. One got the feeling, staring into those eyes, that he'd watched the dice roll at the foot of the cross.

Directly across from Carter was the head of AXE, David Hawk. He was a stocky, white-haired man whose head was usually obscured in mist from a cheap cigar. It was no different now, but the eyes gleaming through the gray fog were much like Shelbain's.

The only difference was, David Hawk had probably won the dice game.

Hawk was bringing the table up to date.

"I won't go into all the crap that Koulami has pulled

in the past. That's practically common knowledge. What we think he's up to now is what we're concerned with this morning.''

He shuffled papers, passed copies around the table, and went on.

''We might not have tumbled to a connection if Shakib Koulami hadn't bought it at Trapur. The raid was well planned and perfectly executed. They must have sized everything for weeks before pulling it off.''

''What did they get?'' Carter asked, preferring to get his information quickly rather than wade through all of the papers before him.

Peterson replied. ''Four lead-lined casks of nuclear reactor fuel.''

''How did they get it out?'' LeMoine asked.

''By helicopter,'' Hawk growled. ''A shady character named Morgan Pawley ran a flying service south of Bombay. He's dead. A hypodermic loaded with cyanide in the neck. Bartender at one of the local hotel watering holes remembers he picked up a woman earlier that night. Pawley was going to give her a look at the sights of Bombay by night.''

''The woman lifted the helicopter?''

''We assume so. The young man who wasted Shakib Koulami swears it was a woman at the controls. From the bartender's description, and the fact that the woman was a pilot and was probably close to Koulami, we've come up with a name. Rami Sherif. Find pictures A and B in your stack.''

Carter found them.

The first photograph showed a beautiful dark-haired girl of about sixteen. She was in a bathing suit with the sea behind her. She had a fine, long nose, wavy black hair, and black eyes that looked coquettishly over her shoulder at the camera. Her figure was full to the point of voluptuousness, with long legs, high breasts, and athletic tone.

The second photo was more formal. In it she wore a mauve, low-cut cocktail dress. She was a little older in this one. Now there was a frank look in her eyes, unafraid and unimpressed by the camera.

The biggest difference between the two photos, besides the clothing and location, was in the eyes. In the second photo the coquettishness was gone. It was replaced with hard cruelty.

Hawk was speaking again. "There were two other raids pulled off within twenty-four hours and in practically the same manner. Peterson?"

"One was in the United States . . . Tennessee, to be exact. They got five canisters of high-grade plutonium. In knowledgeable hands that's a little more than enough to build two bombs."

LeMoine groaned.

"The other strike was in England, at the atomic research facility in Sussex. Whoever did it was a computer expert. Once they got the codes, he knew just what to go for in the memory banks and how to get it out."

"What was the damage there?" Carter asked.

"The plans for a new, improved, and speedier way of converting nuclear waste into raw plutonium. They also obtained the shipping codes and access numbers for the computers at the Lake Athabasca uranium mines in Saskatchewan."

Hawk chimed in. "We have alerted the Canadian government. Security has been doubled and the codes changed."

"How do you know just what they got out of the computer?" Shelbain asked, his voice coming out in a cigarette-and-whiskey-induced growl.

"Luckily," Peterson replied, "a monitor was installed only a few days ago on the printers. We know everything they printed out. Besides the information on Athabasca and the nuclear plants, they also printed out the center's personnel file."

There was a several-second silence around the table, eventually broken by Hawk.

"Gentlemen, I think we can make some pretty clear deductions from all of this. They have the makings to create a bomb—or two—right now. They have the fuel to kick off a reactor to create nuclear waste. And they have the plans to convert that waste into plutonium to build future bombs. And I think we all know who Koulami works for."

Carter took a deep drag on his cigarette and expelled it slowly through his nostrils as he spoke.

"Iran wants the bomb."

François Shelbain and LeMoine brought the rest of them up to date on Paris.

The equipment left behind in the hotel room had been traced back to West Germany. All of it, plus the automobiles, had been stolen weeks before.

The owners and staff of the Café Marie were clean. It had only been used as a drop.

The man killed outside the hotel had been identified as Yuval Heikal, a longtime associate of Amin Koulami. Other than an Islamic medallion around his neck, the body was clean.

The Babolini passport was a good forgery. It, along with the arms, was probably supplied by Allad Khopar.

"Also, Nick," LeMoine added, "you were right about the powder in the compact. It was laced with pheno. They don't miss a trick.''

Carter turned to Shelbain. "What about Khopar? Have your people gotten anything out of him?"

"Nothing, and it's impossible to find his real records. The warehouse in Marseille has been gone through inch by inch. Everything we turned up has been legally invoiced. You can bet there are illegal arms stored somewhere, but our chances of finding them are one in a million. He's being transferred to Toulouse this morning for arraignment on the dope charge, but you know how much chance we have of making that stick.''

"All right," Hawk declared, lighting a fresh cigar, "we might have something. I've gone over the tape of your session with Dr. Rudder this morning, Nick. There are some things on it that might give us a leg up.''

He hit the play button on the tape machine at his elbow, and Carter's voice, sleepily droning but clear, filled the room.

"Needle . . . and the radio . . . Koulami's voice and a woman, spoke in both French and Arabic . . ."

Long silence, then Rudder's voice, urging: *"The voices, what did they say? Can you remember as close to verbatim as possible what they said?"*

A short pause and then Carter's drone again: *"Uh . . . he is with Allah . . . Brussman . . ."*

"Is Brussman the woman or one of the other men in the room?"

"No . . . Brussman's whereabouts, learned Brussman's whereabouts. Will meet Brussman . . . no meet us in three days' time . . ."

Hawk cut the machine. "We put the name through the computer and came up with Dr. Josef Brussman. He's one of the three top nuclear physicists at the Sussex atomic research facility in England.''

LeMoine snapped his fingers. "That's why they wanted the personnel list!"

"Exactly," Hawk said. "Brussman is rather unique among his fellows. He is not only one of the top nuclear physicists in the world, he is also an accomplished engineer."

"Jesus," Carter muttered. "Not only can the guy build a bomb for them, he can construct a reactor."

"It would appear that's why they have pinpointed him. The top people in Sussex are required to leave word at all times as to their status and location. Right now Dr. Brussman, his daughter Eliza, and his assistant, Peter Donahue, are attending a scientific convention in Alexandria. When the convention is concluded they plan on taking a three-week vacation cruising the Nile, touring the ruins, and seeing Cairo."

"They're going to snatch them!" Carter hissed.

"I'd say that, Nick. We have contacted MI6 in London. They are sending a three-man team right now. Her Majesty's government is not the least bit averse to you joining them. Are you up to it?"

"More than up to it, sir."

Hawk leaned forward, the cigar grinding between his teeth. "Nick, I want Koulami. I want the bastard's ears."

Just then an aide popped through the door and moved to François Shelbain's chair. He leaned close to the SDECE chief's ear and whispered.

The man's face clouded. He nodded, dismissing the aide, and looked gravely around the table.

"Gentlemen, a half hour ago in Marseille a sniper killed Allad Khopar with four bullets from a high-powered rifle."

Koulami, Carter thought, *doesn't miss a trick.*

SEVEN

It was a small boat to be out so far, but the man and woman handling it knew exactly what they were doing. Behind them the coast road ran picturesquely along the Egyptian Riviera. To their left, the buildings of Alexandria gleamed in the hot Mediterranean sun. Green rolling hills and sun-scorched beaches ran west as far as the eye could see.

They had left a tiny marina in Alexandria nearly two hours earlier and were now directly in front of Maamura Beach about two miles out.

Selwa Rajon slipped off the white slacks and shirt she was wearing and folded them in the well of the boat over her shoes. Then she pulled the black wet suit top on over her bathing suit and turned to the man at the tiller.

"Kamal . . ."

"Yes, Selwa?"

"Help me with the tanks?"

On his knees behind her, he lifted the tanks until she could slide her arms through the shoulder straps. He helped adjust them and then fit the heavy utility belt around her hips.

"The weight of the belt will tire you fast, Selwa. Be careful."

She chuckled. "It will be much lighter on the swim back out."

After a final check of her air lines and the rest of the equipment, she fit her face mask and slipped over the side. It was cold but not cold enough to impede movement. She loosened the valve to give herself a little more air, and dived under the surface of the sea.

The water was deep and clear. Rays of sunshine angled down through it, giving off a glow of soft light. Fish that darted away when she first splashed into the water reappeared to swim along with her.

Breathing through the mouth, usually awkward, became natural after just a few strokes. When her arms began to tire, she gave them a rest at her sides and used only the powerful thrust of her kicking feet in the flippers.

When the first shadows of land appeared on the surface, she came up. Her head, dark in the rolling water, barely broke the surface.

She got her bearings and dived again.

Now she distanced herself, a yard and a half with each smooth, untiring stroke.

Again she came up, this time three hundred yards offshore on a direct line with the villa and its private pier. Moored to the pier was an eighty-five-foot, three-decked floating palace of the *Moira* class. Her sides gleamed white in the sun, and the polished brass on her decks sparkled.

By narrowing her eyes, Selwa Rajon could read the name and home port. Her name was *Darvais Pride*, printed on the stern in both English and Arabic. Just beneath it was the home port, Manama, the capital of Bahrain.

Quickly, Selwa's trained eyes took in everything. There were three armed guards: one on the foredeck, one aft, and one in the wheelhouse. There were two more at the top of the steps leading from the gardens behind the villa down to the pier.

She let the weight of the belt take her under again; and let the light and dark reflections off the surface tell her when she had reached the yacht's hull.

Around her belt were eight self-contained bombs. Seven contained two pounds of C-4 explosive in a hermetically sealed steel box; one held much less. Attached to each was a smaller Teflon-coated box holding a two-channel receiver. The receivers were in miniature, the same kind found in the fuselage of radio-controlled model airplanes.

Two conductor rods, the area around them also sealed, connected the dual boxes. The inner cores of the rods were the antennae detonators that would blow the C-4.

Carefully, starting just forward of the stern, she placed each explosive device approximately ten feet apart. The casings themselves were magnetized so that all it took on the woman's part was a slight rub, a bit of friction against the hull, and the bombs held fast.

In the eighth and final bomb there was also a tiny beeper device that could be monitored from miles away with a small directional finding unit. She did not arm the detonators. This would be done when the time came by a separate send unit.

A half hour later, Selwa Rajon climbed back into the boat and sprawled, spent, on the bottom.

"Done?"

"Done," she replied, absently stroking her body through the wet suit. "Hurry, let's get back. I can't wait to tell Amin!"

• • •

The customs inspector flipped through Carter's special diplomatic passport, stamped it, and handed it back with a slight bow.

"Have an enjoyable time in Cairo, Mr. Carter."

"Thank you."

Carter got his bag from the VIP gate and walked immediately to the bank window where he converted one thousand American dollars into Egyptian pound notes.

From there he went to the rental car desk and gave his name to the clerk.

"How long will you be needing the car, sir?"

"It's difficult to say. Perhaps several days. Can I drop it off in Alexandria?"

"I can make note of it."

"Do that."

He had taken Pan Am through Rome to Cairo International. He could have flown Cairo to Alexandria via United Arab Airlines, but there were a couple of stops he wanted to make between the two cities.

The Killmaster signed the forms, showed his international driver's license, and paid the deposit in cash. A valet escorted him to the parking lot and opened the door of a four-door, dark blue Cortina.

Carter tipped him, threw his bags into the rear seat, and drove the traffic maze until he was free of the airport. After only one wrong turn he found the Alexandria highway and headed north.

He drove for nearly an hour, glancing often into the rearview mirror to make sure he wasn't being followed.

It was unlikely that Koulami would have the Cairo airport tabbed, but Carter was naturally cautious.

The explosion of the car had been purposely played down in the Paris newspapers. The report did state that two bodies had been discovered in the aftermath of the inferno, a man and a woman, both burned beyond identification.

Koulami had no reason to believe that Carter was still alive, let alone in Egypt.

At the halfway point, he stopped at a small village oasis. It was a combination gas station, run-down hotel, bar, restaurant, and way station for desert traders heading west to east toward the Nile.

This was only too evident, comparing the front and rear of the buildings. There were several large trucks and older model cars parked in front. In the rear were stables filled with camels, horses, and various other livestock. A hundred yards beyond the stables, several brightly colored and festooned tents had been erected.

Carter locked the car and generously tipped the old, toothless car guard before going inside.

Except for some of the merchandise, the first room could have been a country general store in America. To the right was a restaurant. In the rear was a small bar modeled after an English pub.

Carter entered the bar and ordered a small dish of kabob and a local beer. "Do you have a telephone?"

"We do. On the wall there. To where do you call?"

"Alexandria."

"You will need change."

Carter passed over several pound notes and got a handful of coins in return.

He took a long swallow from the beer when it came, lit a cigarette, and strolled back to the phone.

The operator answered in Arabic. Carter switched her to English and asked for an Alexandria number. He deposited half his coins as he listened to an odd ringing tone on the other end of the line.

A low, sultry voice answered in Arabic.

"Do you speak English?" Carter asked.

"Yes. This is Djabi Import/Export. May I help you?"

"Yes, this is an old friend. I would like to speak to Abu, please."

"Neither Mr. Djabi nor his son is in the office at the present time. Would you care to leave a message?"

"Yes, would you tell Djabi senior that Carter is calling? I have a bit of an emergency and it is imperative that I see him this evening, as early as possible."

"Could I have your number, please? I will pass your message along."

Carter gave her the number. "And if he has any doubts, tell him 'the Kufra connection.' "

"I will tell him, sir."

Carter hung up and returned to his beer and kabob.

Abu Djabi had started out as a thief in Cairo God-only-knew how many years before. By the time the war ended and the British had departed, he had become the Prince of Thieves.

With his riches he had sent his two sons to school in England and France. By the time they returned, things had changed. Thievery and smuggling were not as lucrative. The younger Djabis took their father's vast wealth and parlayed it into an even bigger, legitimate fortune.

But the old man couldn't give up the habits of his past. Or his contacts.

When Carter had needed arms and men for a rescue caravan into Kufra, Libya, years before, Kjabi had supplied them . . . for a price, of course.

Ten minutes later the phone rang. The bartender started for it and Carter headed him off.

"Yes?"

"Is this Carter? . . . Nick Carter?"

The Killmaster recognized the voice. "It is Abu. Do

you still have your mother buying and selling camels?''

"Ah, sadly, she is now with Allah and I must be satisfied with a Mercedes. What brings you to Egypt?''

"A slight problem.''

"Like Kufra?''

"No, not like Kufra at all. Do you still have as many eyes and ears in Cairo and Alexandria as you did in the old days?''

"Probably more,'' the old man said and chuckled. "Our present economy makes thieves, and to join the brotherhood one must still consult me. Where are you?''

"Najimbi.''

"An hour from Alexandria.''

"Yes.''

"Do you remember how to find me?''

"I think so.''

"I shall be waiting, old friend. Oh, you did bring money, of course?''

"Of course.''

"No matter. Your credit is good. *Shalom*.'' He chuckled again. "We say that often now, since we have made our peace with the Jews.''

"*Shalom*,'' Carter replied with a laugh. Djabi had traded with Israel all through both wars. He, of all Egyptians, wanted peace with the Israelis. He often told Carter that it was sheer stupidity to kill one's neighbors when a profit could be made from keeping them alive. Carter walked back to the bar, finished his drink, paid, and left.

Outside in the car he opened a street map of Alexandria, checked his route, and with a last glance in the mirror drove north into the gathering dusk.

Peter Donahue walked into the casino room of the

Cecil Hotel, idly stacking and restacking the chips in his hands. But gambling was the last thing on his mind.

Oh, yes, he would gamble, and he would probably lose. But wins or losses didn't interest him.

The woman did. He had thought of nothing but her for the last twenty hours, since they had shared a drink the night before.

He had started out seated across from her at a "21" table. When she had moved to one of the baccarat tables, Donahue had followed.

She had drawn him like a magnet. He had taken the chair next to hers and absently placed a bet. Against all odds, he had won.

Later, around one in the morning when the tables had started to thin out, he had asked her to share a nightcap with him.

Much to his amazement, she had said yes.

She was the most enchanting woman he had ever met. Even when she had mentioned that she was married, Donahue had not been put off.

"May I see you again? Tomorrow?"

"But of course, Peter," she had replied before stepping into her car. "I will be at the same baccarat table."

He wound his way slowly through the roulette and "21" tables toward the high rollers' area where the four tables, for chemin de fer and baccarat, waited.

And then he saw her. If anything she was more mysterious, desirable, and beautiful than he remembered.

Peter Donahue had known many beautiful women, but this one's allure was deeper than mere beauty. Every movement of her body was sensuous, each motion of her hands as she placed her chips called attention to her utter femininity.

She seemed to sense his approach and smiled know-ingly up at him, barely revealing bright, even teeth through her full, sensuous lips.

"Good evening, monsieur. I thought that you might have had a change of mind."

"Never. May I?"

"Of course."

She made a three-quarter turn toward him and Peter Donahue felt blood rush to his face.

She was draped in loose folds of golden metallic net-ting. The mesh was so delicate and intricate that the in-itial impression was of an absence rather than the presence of cloth. This glittering gossamer was abun-dantly arrayed in overlapping layers to form a volumi-nous, transparent nongarment.

"I hope, Peter," she murmured, leaning toward him, "that you can change my luck. The table, thus far, has been very cold."

"I'll try," Donahue replied, barely managing to keep the tremor from his voice. "I will sincerely try."

"Good," she said, returning her concentration to the table.

As she moved, the soft rectangles in the material became distorted and a chain of barbaric necklaces jangled enticingly in front of her full breasts.

Donahue could not be sure if he was occasionally glimpsing the pinkness of nipples or not. He had a feel-ing that he probably was, and blood surged into his temples and his groin.

"Ah!" she cried suddenly, rocking back in her chair and clapping her hands. "We both win!"

"I have changed your luck."

"For the better!" she said. "Come, we double our bet this time."

"Whatever you wish," he mumbled, and leaned closer to her. "Do you know, I never even asked you your name last night."

"No? Well, what is a name?" She shrugged. "My name is Rami."

The Killmaster parked two blocks from his destination in the little village just on the fringe of Alexandria. He got out of the car, took his briefcase, and locked the doors, all without haste.

Somewhere, someone was watching his progress. It was best not to hurry or make any sudden moves.

He looked up and down the village street. The old whitewashed houses and their red roofs glinted in the stark moonlight. It had once been *the* street in the suburbs populated by colonial British.

There was not a soul in sight. Carter's heels, as he made his way along the street, echoed in the lonely night.

At the corner he looked up, over a tall wrought-iron wall. He could see flickering light shining from two of the upstairs windows where the curtains had been drawn. All the rest of the building was in darkness, silent like the street around him.

Carter glanced through the fence at the grounds. The few trees left were gnarled and neglected. Their fruit was rotting. A sandstone lane led up to the house. It had long ago lost its fight with weeds. On both sides of the lane, palms, oleander, and hibiscus bushes grew in junglelike profusion. The trunks of the trees were choked with vines. The smell of night-blooming flowers hung heavy in the still air.

He walked toward the rear of the estate and found a rusty but well-locked gate. He was about to put his finger to the buzzer, when they appeared like ghosts from the shadows.

There were three of them, two inside the gate, one outside, right at Carter's elbow. All of them had sawed-off shotguns slung over their shoulders and pistols stuck in the front of their belts.

"Identify yourself, quickly," one hissed.

"Carter. I have an appointment to see Abu Djabi."

Without a word, the one beside him lifted Carter's arms and patted him down while the other two unlocked and opened the gate. He was relieved of the briefcase and led through a foul-smelling arbor. At the end of it, an open door materialized.

One of the men took his briefcase and motioned Carter to follow. He was led up a flight of stairs and down a landing.

"In here!"

Carter entered a room where only the bedding had been changed since the house had been built in mid-Victorian days.

"Ah, my friend, what I can see of you has not changed since last we met!"

Carter had to blink several times in the dim light before he saw the huge bulk of Abu Djabi near the bed. He was perched on a special chair, not unlike a throne, that had been specially constructed to handle his four-hundred-pound bulk.

Wriggling on the huge man's lap was a curvaceous blonde not more than eighteen.

"I see you still prefer everything but your women old and musty."

Djabi roared with laughter and ended up coughing. "One does not change what one is accustomed to."

"And the security?"

"Also an old habit. I doubt if anyone still wants to kill me, but habits die hard. Sit, sit. A brandy?"

"Scotch."

"Scotch it is." He flapped his enormous jowls at the man with the shotgun. The briefcase was placed close to Djabi's hand and the man headed to a small bar.

"I must say, Carter, your call came at an excellent time. I grow old and bored sitting here waiting to die. Talk to me!"

Carter hesitated, inclining his head toward the girl.

"The girl speaks nothing but German." Djabi shrugged. "I import them for my rich friends in Cairo."

"Nevertheless . . ."

"Very well." Djabi affectionately patted the blonde's bottom and shoved her away, murmuring to her in German. She rolled from his lap, threw a glare at Carter, and jiggled from the room.

Carter accepted the proffered scotch and watched the man who had brought it fade into the shadows.

"He, of course, will have to stay," Djabi said flatly.

"You mean, Abu, that after all this time you still do not trust me?"

Another roaring laugh. "Of course not, old friend. But your tally of kills is every bit as impressive as mine. I did not survive these many years because I trusted the human species . . . friend or foe. Now, tell me what is on your mind. I am hungry for intrigue!"

As the fat man leaned forward intently, his jowls spread in a wide smile, an odd thought crossed Carter's mind.

This was the best Sidney Greenstreet imitation he had ever seen.

EIGHT

Amin Koulami replaced the telephone, a satisfied grin on his face. He reached for his cigarettes but paused when the door opened behind him.

Selwa Rojan stepped into the room.

"It's done," she whispered. "All eight of the mines are attached."

"Excellent. That was Bahrain. Everything arrived safely and awaits us there."

"Amin . . ."

Her voice was husky and her eyes were cloudy. Koulami smiled. He knew this mood; he could read it in all his women.

"You please me greatly, Selwa," he murmured.

She stood facing him and took off her blouse. As the garment fell free, she put her hands under her breasts and lifted them toward him.

"Yes, Selwa . . . go on!"

She unzipped her slacks and let them drop to the floor. Amin let his robe slip from his shoulders and he moved toward her.

Selwa's hot black eyes looked at him with peculiar intensity, as if making a judgment. Then suddenly she slid her arms around his neck. Her beautiful, almost hard face tilted to his as she urged her lips forward. She crushed them against his, at the same time forcing her full breasts into his chest. She kissed him wildly, defiantly. It was a long, sensuous kiss, meant to inflame. At last she pulled away from him.

With a growl, Amin threw her across the bed. She began to hum softly. With another growl he covered her body with his, his lips whispering against her flesh. At the same time, he felt a second pair of hands caress his back. He looked up.

"Rami."

She stood above them both, the same dull glitter in her eyes that he had seen in Selwa's.

"Donahue?"

"He is like a child, a little boy." She smiled. "We have a rendezvous tomorrow evening."

"He agreed to the place?"

"Yes. I told him we must avoid my husband."

Amin laughed. "Join us, Rami. We will celebrate together, the three of us."

Seconds later, Rami Sherif was also nude. And soon after that, all three of them were entwined together on the bed.

The old Egyptian was smart and wily. Age had diminished neither his cunning nor his ability to bargain. It took three hours for Carter to settle on a deal.

Djabi's contacts were more numerous than any police or military force. The three hundred photos of Rami Sherif, and the like number of composite drawings of

Amin Koulami made up from Carter's memory, would go out all over Egypt in a matter of hours.

The Killmaster hoped that one of them would be spotted before they could put their plan—whatever it was—into high gear.

Also, word would go out from the old house in the Alexandria suburbs, and Carter would have three hundred beggars and thieves at his command should he need them.

Carter shared a last glass with the fat old thief, turned down an offer to rest the night in Djabi's harem, and returned to his car.

In Alexandria, he stopped and made a second phone call. His contact was Harlan Effredge, MI6. The phone was answered on the first ring, and the Killmaster was given directions to the safe house they had rented as base headquarters for the operation.

A half hour later, Carter found it in the old section of wealthy residences near the beach. It was still owned by a wealthy British shipowner, and had been commandeered for the occasion by MI6.

Effredge himself met Carter at the door and took his bag. He was led down a hallway lit by wall sconces that appeared to have been only recently converted to electricity. The hallway wound its way through the house until, at last, they entered what once must have been the library.

A fire had been laid to ward off the chill desert night. Effredge set Carter's bag by the fireplace and, without asking, fixed both of them drinks.

"Cheers," he said, handing over one of the glasses.

"Let's hope so," Carter replied, downing a third of the drink in one swallow. "Where are we?"

The MI6 man eased himself into one of the large overstuffed chairs by the fireplace and assembled his thoughts.

"The Egyptians will cooperate, but, needless to say, they're not happy about it. They still don't have a lot of trust in their bones toward us Brits."

Carter nodded his understanding. That was the major reason he had sought help from the old master thief, Abu Djabi. "How many do we have?"

"You, me, and two more of my people . . . Livingstone and Hart-Davis. I believe you've worked with Hart-Davis before."

"Yeah, about a year ago, in London. Good man."

"The whole party is staying at a villa called The Winds on Maamura Beach. It's owned by a high-flying banker named Fawzi Quadhima. He's from Bahrain. His wife's name is Meila. She's Egyptian, and they are both extremely wealthy."

"Are they on the premises?"

"No, but they are flying in day after tomorrow when the scientists finish their meeting. I guess the fun and their holiday starts then."

"How many people are staying at the villa?" Carter asked.

"Let's see. . . . Five brought their wives. Brussman is a widower, but his daughter is with him, and his associate. The Egyptians have insisted that they handle security at the villa."

"So you and your people are relegated to organize-and-watch?"

Effredge shrugged. "That's about it. Fawzi Quadhima has his own bullyboys. I must say, they are good, but, as you know, so is Koulami."

Carter freshened his drink and returned to the welcome warmth of the fireplace. "Have you spoken to Brussman?"

"Yes, told him the whole story."

"And?"

"And he considers it a bloody pain in the ass. This is the first holiday he's had in years and he plans to enjoy it."

"He doesn't want watchdogs."

"That's about it," the MI6 man replied. "But he's getting them whether he likes it or not every time he leaves the villa. We've also got a man with the daughter."

"Eliza, isn't it?"

"Right. She's a little more cautious, more than willing to accept the extra protection."

"Have you pitched her about me?"

"I did. She's willing to meet you and discuss it. She just doesn't know if her father will buy the instant American boyfriend bit."

"But she's willing to try it?"

Effredge nodded and checked his watch. "You're to meet her at the Neferet, a supper club."

"I know it," Carter replied, and moved to the tall windows. He gazed out at the twinkling lights of Alexandria and frowned in concentration. "What time?"

"About an hour. She's having dinner with the assistant, Donahue."

"What about him?"

"We don't have anybody on him, if that's what you mean. He's more a social secretary for Brussman than anything else, and not privy to any official secrets or the old man's work."

"How close are he and the daughter?"

"Not very. Donahue acts as her escort now and then.

She and the old man are close to him, but Donahue is a bit of a playboy on his own time."

"Just had a thought," Carter said, moving back to the fireplace and standing over the other man.

"Yes?"

"What if it isn't Brussman? What if it's someone else?"

"We've thought of that. It's not likely. Brussman has the expertise in several fields Koulami needs if he wants to build both a bomb and a reactor. The others don't. Besides, Nick, covering Brussman and the daughter is one hell of a job. Putting a blanket over all of them would be damned close to impossible under these conditions."

"Yeah," Carter growled. "Why in hell did they have to hold their little soiree in the Middle East?"

"Quadhima is big on nuclear power for peace. He sponsored it." He glanced at his watch. "You'd better move if you're going to meet the lady."

Carter nodded and headed for the door. He was halfway down the hall when the phone in the room he had just left started ringing.

A sixth sense made him pause and wait. Two seconds later, Effredge stuck his head through the door.

"Nick, for you!"

If it wasn't Washington, it could only be one person.

"Carter here."

"A croupier at the Cecil Hotel casino thinks he may have spotted your woman this evening," Abu Djabi replied.

"That's fast work."

Djabi wheezed out a laugh. "That's why you came to me, my friend. His name is Hashan. His shift ends just before midnight. Where do you want to meet him?"

Carter went over Alexandria in his mind. "The Mockdar."

"Agreed."

The phone went dead in Carter's ear.

"Something?"

"Let's hope so," Carter replied, and headed for the door.

The Neferet was a quaint little place sitting on the edge of a cliff overlooking the ocean. From the road it was almost hidden in a grove of trees.

Carter handed his keys to one of Ali Baba's thieves and entered the bar. He spotted Jonathan Hart-Davis at the bar and slipped onto the stool beside him.

"Jon."

"Nick. Welcome to the circus."

"Effredge clued me in. Brussman and daughter don't like company."

Hart-Davis shrugged and sipped his drink. "The old man's a pain. The daughter's not so bad, but she does what he says."

"Where is she?"

"In the dining room. You can't miss her."

"Peter Donahue with her?"

"No, he slipped away right after dinner. He's probably at the Cecil, gambling."

"I'll take her for the rest of the night if you want a break."

"Appreciated."

Carter took his drink and ambled into the dining room. There were only three single women. One was a dowager, another a mousy schoolteacher type who looked as though she wished she had never left her classroom.

Eliza Brussman was easy to spot.

Carter had somehow expected a long-legged blonde with flaring nostrils and haughty porcelain features and cold blue eyes.

She was quite the opposite, with chestnut brown hair worn short and warm hazel eyes. Her features weren't refined, but she had her own beautiful, very natural sort of charm, with a turned-up nose that was slightly broad in an almost completely round face.

Carter was nearly to the table when she sensed his presence and turned to face him.

"Eliza Brussman?"

"Yes?"

Her lips were full, sensuous, and she had a tiny cleft in her chin. Her eyes were large and expressive, possessing a sort of innocence that belied her earthy nature.

Her smile was genuine as she offered her hand. He took it, and was surprised at its firmness.

"I'm very pleased to meet you, Mr. Carter. Do sit down."

The Killmaster glanced around. The tables near them were filling up for the late show. "If you don't mind, I'd like to discuss this on the terrace."

"Of course," she said easily, and stood.

Her voice had a sexual huskiness to it that didn't fit the face or the wide smile. It did fit the rest of her.

She was tall, at least five-nine, and wore a moss green raw silk suit, the jacket thrust open by high breasts beneath a beige blouse.

"Are we surrounded by terrorists?" she asked, taking his arm and letting a glint of amusement flash into her eyes.

"We might be," he replied without humor.

The terrace was empty. Carter stopped at the rail, set

his drink down, and lit a cigarette. She shook her head when he offered her one.

"Quite a view," she said.

The terrace seemed to hang on the edge of the cliff. There was a hundred-foot drop to the water below.

"Be a nice place to commit suicide."

She looked at him sharply but saw only coldness in his eyes and a bland grin.

"Why do you say that?"

"Because that's what your father may be doing if he doesn't cooperate with us."

Her shoulders sagged and the amusement left her eyes. "I've tried to talk to him."

"But he won't listen?"

"No. Perhaps if you—"

"No, I would rather he didn't know who I am." He fished in his pocket and handed her a cable. "You received this earlier this evening. I arrive on the noon flight tomorrow. You met me in New York when you were there two months ago. We had a brief fling and you very much want to reignite the flame. That's why you would like to invite me to stay at the villa."

Only the corners of her mouth curled in a smile. "Do you think my father will buy this?"

"I think so. You're thirty-two. You've been married and divorced twice. Since your last divorce two years ago, you have had several affairs, two of them quite torrid. I think he'll accept it."

Her face flushed. "My God, you've been spying on me!"

"Not really. Your life is a fairly open book and you haven't exactly tried to hide anything."

The smile broadened as she took in his tall, muscular frame and the scarred, darkly tanned features.

"Father might accept you at that. I'm sure you would appeal to him more than the men I've picked thus far." Suddenly her eyes narrowed and the smile dropped away. "Now, suppose you tell me everything. Effredge just said we were in danger of being kidnapped. He really wouldn't say why."

Carter hesitated, studying her. It was a professional appraisal, and he approved of what he saw. The suddenly tight clasp of her hands, the nervous look in her eyes, the firm set of her mouth. Sincerity.

"All right, perhaps you should know it all."

It took him nearly twenty minutes to bring her completely up to date. He left nothing out, including Allad Khopar's assassination, the thefts of the nuclear materials, and the cold-blooded killing of the woman in Paris by Koulami to save himself.

By the time he had finished, Eliza's face was white and Carter had little doubt that she would cooperate.

"My God, why didn't Effredge tell us this in the first place?" she gasped.

"He did tell your father. And he was told by your father not to alarm you."

"I'll do anything you ask."

"Good. At breakfast, notify everyone of my arrival. Do it rather breathlessly, as if you can't wait." He glanced at his watch. It was eleven-fifteen. "Right now I'm taking you home."

"But it's early . . . all right."

The sudden meekness was no act. Carter was sure of it. Eliza Brussman was scared.

In the rented Cortina, he drove in silence for several minutes. When he was away from the city and on the coast road, he finally spoke.

"Why did your escort leave you alone tonight?"

"Peter?"

"Yes."

"The casino. He loves to gamble. And I think he's met a woman." Here she laughed. "He usually does, wherever he goes. Peter is a very sexual person."

"Anything between the two of you?"

"None of your business."

"The hell it isn't," he snapped. "Everything is my business now."

She pouted, but spoke at last. "Nothing. Peter has been with my father for years. We're more like brother and sister. I care for him a great deal, as does my father, but that is as far as it goes. Besides, he's not really my type."

Carter chuckled. "What is your type?"

Her laugh in reply was low and throaty. "Maybe I'll let you know before all this is over."

Carter let her off at the gates of the villa, made sure she was safely inside, and headed back to Alexandria.

At five minutes before twelve he parked across from the Mockdar. Carter had been there before, several times. The first floor was a seedy club that closed every morning at dawn for an hour to be swept out. The three floors above it held an opulent brothel.

Besides catering to gentlemen who were looking for ladies of the evening, the club drew all the bartenders from the other clubs, croupiers and dealers from the casinos, and women who would rather free-lance than live in.

Midnight was the magic hour. The front bar was crowded, keeping three bartenders and twice as many scantily clad waitresses busy. Near the stairs leading to the upper floors, a stony-faced madam checked anyone coming through the door as a potential customer.

She took one quick look at Carter and glanced away.

The Killmaster entered the rear room and squinted through the smoke until he could make out faces. He was pretty sure he spotted his man in the last booth near the wall.

Their eyes met as Carter approached. Thieves have a look the world over. Even in a tuxedo with a frilly shirt and perfectly manicured nails, this one had the look.

"Hashan?"

"Yes."

"I am Carter. Abu tells me you have good eyes."

"Sit."

Carter slid into the booth and ordered local beer. They made small talk until it came and the waitress had retreated. Then the little Egyptian leaned forward and lowered his voice.

"The woman in the picture—I have seen her the last two nights at the casino."

"The Cecil?"

"Yes."

"Are you sure?"

"I, myself, took her reservation tonight for a chair at the baccarat table."

"In what name?"

He fished a piece of paper from his pocket. "Monique Hoseini. The name checked against her passport."

"What local address did she list on her casino entrance card?"

"The Sheraton," Hashan replied. "I called to check. They have no one by that name registered. But that is not unusual. A married woman comes to the casino to gamble or meet men, she does not want her husband to know where she is. It happens often.''

''Was this woman alone?''

''Yes, both last night and tonight. But she flirted with many men at the table.''

''Did anyone leave with her?''

''No, I don't think so.''

Carter thought for a moment. ''Did she make a table reservation for tomorrow night?''

''Yes.''

''You have done well, Hashan,'' Carter replied, squeezing five hundred pounds into the man's hand beneath the table.

Carter dropped another bill on the table to cover the drinks, and left.

Amin Koulami held the acrid smoke from the hashish pipe deep in his lungs until his head began to swim. Then he expelled it slowly while he ran his hands over the naked bodies at his side.

In no time the smoke took effect. He was about to awaken one of the women, when the telephone near his head buzzed.

''Yes?''

''It is Achmed.''

''Yes, my friend, what is it?''

''The woman's bodyguard was changed tonight at the Neferet restaurant. I overheard a little of his talk at the bar. He is an American.''

''What? Are you sure?'' Koulami exclaimed.

''Yes, Amin, I am sure of it.''

Koulami expelled air from his lungs to clear his head. ''I suppose it is natural that they would add an American to the team watching the scientists.''

"I disagree, Amin. I think they suspect something. They are guarding only Brussman and his daughter, I'm sure of it."

"Nonsense, my friend. How could they possibly know? No, this guard is a natural precaution with men of such vast knowledge in a foreign country."

"I am not so sure. We followed—"

"Dammit, Achmed, what have I told you? Stay inconspicuous! The plan is foolproof—follow it!"

"Yes, Amin."

"Good night, Achmed."

Amin Koulami dropped the phone back to its cradle and took a long drag on his pipe. Then he turned on his side.

"Rami . . ." he rasped huskily.

The woman groaned and fluttered her eyes. "Yes?"

"Turn over on your stomach, little one."

Achmed Boudia returned to the car where Ja'il, his brother, awaited him.

"Well?"

"He says do nothing," Achmed grunted. "We are merely to observe."

Ja'il shrugged and flipped his cigarette from the window. "He is the boss."

"I know, but the presence of the American bothers me."

"Perhaps he is an old friend."

"I don't think so. After he talked at the bar with the Englishman, he alone remained with the girl. And why are they watching only Brussman and his daughter? Why not the others and their wives?"

"Achmed, you are an old woman," Ja'il sighed. "Two more days and it will be done. Besides, Amin's plan is so thorough that even if the British knew what we wanted, they would be confused.''

''I'm not so sure . . . the American—''

''Achmed, please. Let us return to the hotel. We have put everyone else to bed, now let us go to bed ourselves.''

''Is the one in the tuxedo still in there?''

''Yes, but . . .''

''We'll wait for him.''

Hashan, the little Cecil Hotel casino croupier, gave Carter a full twenty minutes before he left the Mockdar himself. Outside, he shunned a taxi and walked the few blocks to his apartment.

In the basement of his building was an all-night café that served hot lamb on skewers just off the fire and potent Egyptian wine. It was Hashan's habit to stop in this place every evening after work. He would eat and drink until the wee hours. This served two purposes. He made contacts for his other vocation—that of thief—and he didn't have to go home when his nagging wife was still awake.

He saw no reason to break his habit this night.

''Achmed, it has been two hours. He is in there for the night. Let us go . . .''

''No. I'm going in after him. Get ready to drive!''

''Brother, you are a fool. Amin will peel the skin from both our butts.''

''Not if I am right about the American. He met this one at the Mockdar for a reason. I want to know why.''

Achmed stepped from the car and walked across the street, closing his ears to his brother's exhortations to come back.

When Achmed entered the room he had to pause to let his eyes adjust. The air was heavy with smoke, and there was the sharp odor of hashish and incense.

He saw his quarry at a table at the very end of the bar with his back against the wall. Achmed edged along the bar and sat at the next table.

There were three men at the bar and about a half-dozen men at tables in the center of the room.

All talk stopped when Achmed entered. He saw instantly why. These were men of the night and this was the hole they crawled into. They were thieves, pickpockets, and probably murderers. Achmed had been in places just like this all over the world.

A monster with a shaved head and flowing black mustache and wiping his hands on a filthy apron leaned over the bar and stared into Achmed's face without speaking.

"*Neski*," Achmed said. The glass of potent wine was poured and served. He drank it in one swallow, didn't grimace, and set the glass on the table for a refill. "Tura gives a man a terrible thirst."

At the mention of the dreaded desert prison outside Cairo, the men returned to their drinks and conversation.

Achmed sipped his *neski* and glanced now and then at the man in the tuxedo near him. He had obviously been drinking heavily, and from the hooded eyes Achmed guessed he had also been smoking as much.

"Tura?" the man suddenly exclaimed, opening one eye.

"Yes," Achmed said, nodding.

"How long?"

"Two years . . . of hell."

"Even Allah could not help one survive Tura. I was in there for three years."

"Hell."

"Yes, hell. I am Hashan."

"Murzuk," Achmed lied. "Can I buy you a drink?"

"I would prefer a pipe."

"Of course."

The minutes dragged out until nearly an hour had passed. Achmed was an impatient man. Also, if he waited too much longer, the man called Hashan would pass out and it would take hours to revive him enough for interrogation.

Achmed decided to take a drastic measure.

"Are you awake, my friend?"

"Of course," Hashan slurred.

"Then you know that this is a large-caliber pistol in your belly. I want you to get up and walk just in front of me to the door. When we get there, you will turn and bid good night to your friends. Nod if you understand."

Sweat had popped out in little bubbles all over Hashan's face. He nodded, gasping for breath, and slid from the chair. "Why . . ."

"Just do as I tell you," Achmed said, falling in behind him.

They were just passing the middle of the bar when Hashan whirled. He tried to drive his stiffened fingers into Achmed's throat, but the blow was easily avoided.

The bartender glimpsed the gun and came over the bar in a lunge. Achmed brought the barrel of the big revolver in an arc, down across the man's wrist. The bones exploded in popping sounds, and Achmed grabbed Hashan's arms. He wrenched them up behind the little man's back and shoved him toward the door.

It took a few seconds before a look of realization and pain flashed across the bartender's face. Then he started screaming obscenities and, broken wrist and all, lunged over the bar at Achmed.

Achmed had almost wrestled Hashan to the door when the hairless giant caught up with them.

"You are not police! Where do you take my friend?"

Achmed said nothing. He buried his foot in the man's groin, dropping him instantly.

The other men in the bar had been watching in a state of frozen amazement. It all happened so quickly and so unexpectedly that not one of them moved until the bartender went down. As Achmed dashed into the street, forcefully guiding Hashan, they all ran for the door. But it was effectively blocked by the body of the moaning bartender attempting to rise.

Ja'il saw his brother and the man in the tuxedo. Instantly the car's engine roared to life and the big auto lurched ahead. Coming even with the dim lights from the interior, Ja'il threw open the passenger door so that Achmed didn't have to hesitate as he shoved the little croupier into the rear seat.

"Drive!" Achmed cried, slamming the door behind him.

Ja'il gunned the powerful automobile down the street and around the corner as the men poured from the bar.

"What in God's name do you want?" Hashan cried.

"Answers to questions . . . lots of questions," Achmed hissed.

"Where to, brother?" Ja'il asked from the front seat.

"The desert. Drive far out into the desert," Achmed replied, and turned back to the man beneath him. "You met a man tonight . . . an American. I want his name.

And I want to know of what you talked."

"Nothing, I know nothing!" Hashan replied, twisting his body, trying to heave Achmed's enormous bulk from him.

"You are a thief, a petty thief, little man. Who was the American, and what did he want with you?"

"Nothing, I tell you—"

Hashan's words were throttled in his throat and finally erupted in an agonized scream as Achmed's powerful grip closed around his testicles.

"No! My God, no! *No!*" The little man shrieked in pain, tears streaming at once from his popping eyes.

"Who was the man, the American!"

"I tell you—"

"*Who!*" Achmed hissed, leaning his face close to the other man's and violently squeezing and twisting.

"Carter! The man's name is Carter! He was sent to me by Abu Djabi."

"Good," Achmed replied, squeezing even harder. "Now you'll tell me everything, won't you, little man?"

"Yes, yes! Everything!"

NINE

Eliza Brussman welcomed Carter with open arms and parted lips as he stepped from the cab.

"Good," he whispered, "very good."

"I always thought I would make a great actress," she replied, tickling his earlobe with the tip of her tongue. "Come meet Daddy!"

Daddy turned out to be a little man with hawklike eyes behind thick glasses, rumpled clothes, and stooped shoulders.

In a brief verbal exchange he managed to let Carter know that he didn't approve of him, didn't much approve of *any* of Eliza's friends—particularly male—and considered the American a party crasher.

When those feelings were firmly established, the old man wandered off without so much as a fare-thee-well.

"Well, what do you think?" Eliza said with a chuckle, turning to Carter.

"I think your father has a bad ulcer that gives him a perpetually rotten disposition."

"Chalk it up to genius." She shrugged. "You have to get used to him."

"I'd rather get used to you."

Her laugh was high and clear, and it came as much from her eyes and face as it did from her throat. "We'll work on that later. Now, come along and I'll introduce you to the rest of the menagerie."

The next hour was spent in small talk meeting the other scientists and their wives. Carter forgot the names and most of the faces immediately after moving on to the next couple. He was much more attuned to the Egyptian security people, Quadhima's roving body-guards, and the servants.

Eventually he was able to tug Eliza away from the others. "Were you able to discreetly ask around among the servants?"

She nodded. "Every one of them has been on the staff for years. No one has been hired in the last few weeks."

"Damn, that takes care of that theory," he grumbled. "What's the agenda?"

"Another 'think tank' discussion this afternoon, dinner tonight. That's about it for today."

"And tomorrow?"

"Quadhima and his wife arrive in the morning. Around ten, my father and the others will meet with him to discuss their findings and recommendations for a Mideast nuclear peace foundation. The afternoon is free, and then a farewell dinner on the yacht."

Carter mulled this over. "Is that it?"

Eliza shrugged and nodded. "Day after tomorrow, the holiday begins."

"That's the sightseeing trip to Cairo and down the Nile?"

"No."

"What do you mean, 'no'?" Carter asked, little alarm bells going off in the back of his head.

"My father can't resist mixing business with pleasure. He has accepted Quadhima's offer to cruise through the Suez Canal, down the Red Sea, and around the Gulf of Aden into the Persian Gulf."

"To Bahrain?"

She nodded. "They will inspect the site Quadhima has picked out for the foundation. That has been the plan all along."

"Your father wasn't going to Cairo?"

"No, just Peter and I."

"I see."

Carter excused himself and roamed the estate. He checked the perimeter of the grounds around the villa and the complex of buildings themselves.

Everything was secure. Nothing short of an armed raiding party could get to Josef Brussman here. And Carter was fairly sure that Koulami was not suicidal enough to try that.

He found the yacht equally secure, with armed guards on the decks at all times. Disgruntled, he drifted down to the main salon. It was all polished teak and mahogany, with gilt mirrors, sparkling chandeliers, and gleaming brass.

A full bar covered one entire bulkhead. He was about to fix himself a drink, when he sensed that he wasn't alone.

"May I join you?"

He was tall and angular, with a well-toned body beneath casual clothes. His eyes were the blackest Carter had ever seen. As Carter stared into them, he felt he was looking right through the pupils into the man's soul . . . and it wasn't there.

"I am Mohamed Najjar, head of the Egyptian security team."

Carter shook his hand. "Nick Carter. I—"

"I know who you are, Mr. Carter, and I welcome you. But I must warn you that I and my men have the authority here."

Carter shrugged. "Drink?"

"I don't drink."

"I do." He poured a half tumbler of scotch and dropped a single cube into it. He saluted the other man and sipped. "I admire your security setup here. It's good."

"Thank you."

"What happens when the party's over? When they sail?"

"Then it is out of my hands. I would assure you that Quadhima's people are excellent. Besides the three trained bodyguards, all five members of the *Darvais Pride*'s crew are adept at protecting their master's life."

"Then neither of us has anything to worry about, do we?" Carter said drily.

"Nothing."

Carter disliked this man intensely, but he sensed his strength and his ability. So far he had seen nothing, not a single crack through which Koulami could slip.

Maybe the Iranian terrorist had bitten off more than he could chew. Kidnapping Brussman at the villa or in Alexandria was impossible. Hijacking a heavily armed yacht with trained antiterrorist agents on board would be equally impossible.

Maybe Koulami would pass and look for an easier target.

That would let Carter off the hook for the meantime.

But it would still leave him with the problem of recovering the plutonium and nuclear fuel that had been stolen.

And without Brussman as bait to draw Koulami into the open, that would be a major undertaking.

Najjar was speaking again. "You must understand, Carter, that this situation is a matter of pride to my government. We must establish the fact that we can protect ourselves and any visitors against terrorists."

"Of course." Carter finished his drink and moved around from behind the bar. "A supposition."

"Yes?"

"If Koulami does try it, and you get him, what then?"

"He would be tried according to Islamic and Egyptian law."

Carter nodded and smiled sardonically. "I thought so. Good day, Mohamed Najjar."

The Killmaster stepped out onto the deck into the sun.

If, he thought, *I get to Koulami first, he will be tried according to Carter's law.*

Eliza Brussman dressed carefully for dinner. She paid extra special attention to her hair and her makeup. She was going over her eyes for the fourth time, when it suddenly struck her how much this American, Carter, was affecting her.

They had spent almost the whole afternoon by the pool together. When he finally relaxed, she found him charming and witty.

There had been a trio playing by the pool for afternoon tea. Eliza had practically forced him to dance with her. Carefully, she had turned the conversation to Cairo.

"My father will be well guarded on Quadhima's yacht, won't he?"

"Yes, I think so."

"But I will need someone with me in Cairo."

"I've thought of that. If they can't get to your father, then it would figure you would be the next best target."

"Then you'll come to Cairo with Peter and myself?"

Carter laughed. "I think you're taking all this much too lightly."

"Not at all. Quite the contrary. I'm taking it all very seriously."

She smiled and allowed him to tug her body closer to his. The movement and his proximity affected her at once. There was a sauveness and a Continental polish about this big man, but Eliza sensed a raw power beneath his civilized exterior that sent an odd surge through her body.

He was handsome in a rough sort of way, with blunt, chiseled features and a lopsided grin. His hair was almost black with flecks of gray, and his dark eyes when they openly appraised her alternated between a soft warmth and a look of steel.

Such had always been the case with Eliza. She could tell, almost at first glance, if a man interested her or turned her off. There was a sensual, animal quality combined with a gentle warmth in Nick Carter that definitely attracted her.

She smiled at her reflection in the mirror. Tonight she would find out just how much he attracted her.

A light tap on the door brought her mind back to the room.

"Yes?"

"It's me, Peter. Are you decent?"

"No, but come in anyway."

She wore only a loosely tied robe with nothing beneath it, but with Peter it made little difference.

"Make excuses for me tonight, will you, luv?"

"Peter . . ."

"Don't worry. And don't worry if you don't see me in the morning."

A frown creased Eliza's brow. "Is she married?"

"Yes," he laughed, "so we have to be very discreet."

Eliza shook her head. "One day you'll be shot by a jealous husband."

"Never. I am too careful, my sweet!" He pecked her on the cheek and was gone.

A half hour later one of the maids bustled in with a note.

It was from Carter.

"Make my excuses for missing dinner. Sorry, business. N."

"Damn!" she hissed, thinking how boring the coming evening was going to be listening to one of her father's colleagues, or worse, one of their wives.

Carter had taken a table in the shadows of the mezzanine floor. From there he could see all of the huge room below. Both baccarat tables were directly in his line of sight.

Outside, Harlan Effredge and Jon Hart-Davis were set in separate cars.

But the woman had not shown. Her reserved seat at the number two table had long ago been given up to a paunchy man who appeared too drunk to even ascertain if he were winning or losing.

Carter had been there for three hours. Nothing.

Now it was nearly midnight, and he was almost positive that she wouldn't show.

Carter had spoken to two of the other croupiers, inquiring about Hashan. He hadn't yet shown up for work, but that wasn't unusual. Hashan had other interests that he often took evenings off to pursue.

The Killmaster could guess what those "other interests" were. Some wealthy woman in one of the posh hotels would wake up in the morning without her jewelry.

"Would you care for another drink, sir?"

"No. The check, please."

Carter paid it and made his way through the main room to the lobby. Effredge was lounging by the huge glass doors, smoking.

"*Nada*," Carter said.

"Nothing out here, either. Maybe your man was wrong."

"Could be, but he didn't show up tonight."

Effredge chuckled. "That's not surprising, once you told me who it was."

The MI6 man had been openly dubious when Carter had finally told him about bringing Abu Djabi into the game.

"We might as well knock it off for the night. I'll see you in the morning at the villa. Between the two of us, maybe we can convince Quadhima to let you make the cruise to Bahrain."

Effredge's lips tightened. "If we can't, I'll just have to pull rank and escort Brussman back to England on the Queen's command. *That* he can't say no to."

Carter wasn't so sure of that. Josef Brussman definitely had a mind of his own.

The two men said their good-byes and Carter made his way through the parking lot to the rented Cortina.

•   •   •

Rami's chauffeur had picked Peter Donahue up in the Cecil Hotel's parking lot. He was whisked to a section of Alexandria he had never seen before. But he could have cared less.

He was ushered into an old colonial house from an enclosed courtyard, and she was waiting, standing near a candlelit table set for two.

"What about your chauffeur?"

"He is no problem. I, not my husband, pay his salary."

"Where are we?"

"Does it matter?" she said, leading him to the table.

"No, not at all," he murmured huskily.

She had mesmerized him. The dinner was delicious, though he couldn't wait for it to be finished. Over brandy and strong Egyptian coffee, she made small talk.

Peter Donahue fidgeted.

"You are impatient, my love," she teased, a slow smile curving her provocative lips.

"Does it show so much?" he asked, blushing.

"Yes. But, it is quite flattering. Come, follow me!"

She didn't have to ask twice. He eagerly followed her up a long, curving staircase, down a hall, and into a bedroom. Along the way, Peter Donahue hardly noticed the cobwebs clinging to the ceilings, the dust or the absence of pictures or tapestries on the wall or carpets on the floor.

All his thoughts were on the beguiling woman who led him like a spider into a web.

The bedroom was outrageously primed for his arrival. It was appropriately darkened, a low-banked fire in the fireplace, the only other light provided by strategically scattered candles in the gloom. The drapes were partially opened, and below them Alexandria twinkled and breathed.

More brandy was ready at the glass bar, and the cassette recorder, continually winding its way through a ninety-minute tape, droned out soft, romantic music.

An even more conducive invitation to erotic delights was the unique gown that Rami had chosen. It was a pale pink creation of some diaphanous fabric that covered her body from neck to toes. But it didn't really cover at all, for standing against the light, her naked body was silhouetted perfectly through its loose, flowing folds. Taken head on, when the firelight flared more brightly, the nipples of her breasts were plainly visible through a barely existent bra.

A sash tied at the waist gave the gown a nipped-in trimness. With her hair pinned back, barefoot as she was, she seemed almost innocent and fragile.

"This is very dangerous, what we do," she breathed. "My husband is very rich and powerful."

"Any danger is worth having you," Donahue rasped, sweat soaking his clothing.

Undoing her gown, Rami wiggled her lush body until the garment lay in a heap at her feet like a pink cloud. She stepped out of it, then she took a deep breath and removed the pins from her hair. When it was loose, she shook her head so the thick curls cascaded sensually down around her shoulders and breasts.

She stood like that for a moment, letting his eyes drink in the perfection of her body. Then she breathed deeply, sending the globes of her breasts in twin bulges above the bra. The valley between them was warmly inviting to a kiss or a caress. The nipples had hardened and pushed against the bra's delicate fabric.

"You're a beautiful woman," Peter hissed hotly.

The woman smiled and unhooked the bra and slid it slowly outward over her breasts. They seemed to swell and extend, following the lacy fabric as it came off, until they stood firm, without any sag at all, far in front of her body. Then she reached for her panties.

"Let me," Donahue gasped, kneeling before her.

He was so enraptured as the panties rolled down over her thighs that he hardly felt the biting sting in his neck just behind his right ear.

As the cloud of darkness swam over him, he tried to rise. In so doing, he turned and saw the man in the doorway . . . a short, swarthy man with a pencil-thin mustache across his upper lip.

The husband, Donahue thought. *Oh, my God, the husband!*

And then he passed out.

"You really didn't need to go that far, little one."

Rami Sherif shrugged as she got back into her clothes. "You said you wanted no marks on him. Besides, I enjoyed it."

Amin Koulami sighed and smiled. "I know you did . . . you always do."

"Carter?"

"He is being taken care of at this very moment."

Twenty minutes later, Peter Donahue was in the rear of an ambulance heading south toward Cairo.

TEN

At that hour the coast road was nearly deserted. Carter drove fast, confident of the little car.

He was halfway to the villa before he spotted the headlights behind him coming up fast . . . too fast.

He cursed his wandering mind. There were too many thoughts that had crowded out caution.

After two nights at the casino, why would Rami Sherif not show up tonight?

Why had Hashan not shown up for work?

Why hadn't Effredge and MI6 been told that, after leaving the villa, Brussman was cruising to Bahrain instead of going to Cairo?

But now there was no time to reason. A second pair of headlights appeared in the rearview mirror. They passed the first car and came on strong. It was a big French Citroen. Out of the corner of his eye, Carter could spot just one occupant, the driver.

The Citroen was halfway around Carter's Cortina when the first car nudged his rear bumper. It was a pincer movement and they were pulling it off.

The machine crowding his ass was an old Mercedes, probably built like a tank. There were two men in the front seat, and Carter could spot the barrel of a submachine gun in front of the passenger's face.

Another bounce from the one in the back and the Citroen started squeezing him. Their intent was obvious. At the right time the Citroen would do a brodie in front of him while the old Mercedes crimped him from behind. When that was accomplished, all three would make Swiss cheese out of him and the Cortina.

Ahead lay a two-mile stretch of narrow, twisting, downhill road. It was the most dangerous hunk of concrete between Alexandria and Maamura Beach.

Koulami's hot dogs, if that was who they were, had chosen well.

Metal screamed as the maneuvering began. Carter held his own through the first turn and accelerated into the next.

It was eerie, hearing the sound of so many tires squealing in the otherwise quiet night. Then all three of them were drifting into the final hairpin turn that led to the straight stretch down to the beach. It was 120 degrees to the right and sloped 35 degrees up the last hill.

Halfway into it, the sound of metal grinding against metal drowned out the squeal of tires.

If they are going to move, Carter thought, *this is where they'll do it.*

He was right.

As they thundered out of the last turn, the guy in the Citroen poured the coals to the big black machine.

Carter shifted down for pickup, then back into fourth for speed. His foot felt as if it were caving in the floorboard, but it did little good. The Citroen was just too powerful.

A hundred yards into the straight stretch, the driver of the Citroen slammed on his brakes and lurched into a sideways skid.

Behind Carter, the Mercedes was slowing, waiting for Carter's move.

There were few agreeable options. He could slam into the side of the Citroen and probably put his own head through the Cortina's windshield. He could veer to the right and take a bath in the ocean seventy or so feet below. Or he could go left, climb the embankment, and hope the little car didn't roll on him.

One hell of a short choice.

Arms, feet, and head all worked at once.

He downshifted, braked, and cranked the wheel left. When he felt the Cortina's nose go up he hit the gas again, full.

The little car climbed gallantly. But about halfway up the embankment the rear wheels lost traction. The car began to backslide. As it did, it turned sideways.

Carter felt the tilt, waited until the last minute, and then dived out the door.

The Cortina went over as Carter hit the ground and clawed for a handhold among the desert scrub and rocks.

Below him, all three shooters were out of their cars and peppering the Cortina as it rolled.

The submachine gun was chattering from somewhere close behind the Mercedes. It was joined by the sharp crack of a rifle. The Citroen driver was leveling a magnum over the car's roof, pouring slugs through the Cortina's windshield where Carter should have been.

It was the Citroen man who first spotted Carter. "He's out . . . there on the hill!"

The Killmaster had been trying to reach the top of the

embankment. Being spotted killed that. He dropped to his belly and filled both hands with Wilhelmina.

Two quick shots creased the Citroen's roof, but the shooter had already rolled away.

The submachine gun chattered, sending rock chips and dirt all over Carter's shoulders. He took two rolls to his right and got himself behind some low rocks. They weren't much, but, combined with the darkness, would give him breathing time.

Suddenly there was silence . . . or almost silence.

Far to his right he could hear the sliding, crunching sounds of someone going up the embankment. The second one from the Mercedes was trying to flank him.

Carter chanced a quick look. He could see movement to the rear of the Citroen. A quick shot stopped it, but instantly the machine gun started chattering again, the slugs coming all too close.

When the chatter gun fell quiet, Carter rolled to his back and listened. His straining ears could hear the movement directly above him on the brow of the embankment. He balanced the Luger on his knees and waited.

"Hafiz?" came a voice from below.

"Yes, now!"

The man called Hafiz stood. He fired wildly at the rocks near Carter. For a brief second his body was outlined against the night sky.

In that time Carter pumped two slugs into his chest. There was a gargled scream and the body went sailing down the embankment.

It was the confusion the Killmaster needed.

Both shooters below started firing at the tumbling body. Carter rolled up to his knees and concentrated on the orange flame spurting from the end of the chatter gun.

He aimed above it slightly to the right, and squeezed off the rest of the clip.

The man spun like a top and fell facedown over the hood of the Mercedes.

Carter was on his feet instantly, running in a crouch along the embankment. As he moved he jacked a new clip into the Luger.

He had moved barely in time to avoid a stream of slugs that tore up the earth where he had been a few seconds earlier.

Carter ran hard for twenty yards and then dropped to the road. Silently, in a crouch, he came back until the Mercedes was between him and the last man.

"Stalemate, bastard!" Carter shouted.

The magnum barked, but the slug was several feet to his right, wild.

Carter crawled forward. The machine gun lay where it had fallen near the left front tire of the Mercedes. Still hidden behind the tire and fender, Carter inched his hand forward until his fingers closed over the barrel.

Gingerly but quietly, he pulled it to him.

Now, you bastard, Carter thought, *I've got the fire-power.*

He crawled around the Mercedes and was coming up on the other side when suddenly the Citroen's engine roared to life. The car backed around and the headlights came on, bathing Carter in their glare.

There was no hesitation. He sprayed the headlights and the radiator and then the windshield.

The man was out of the car in an instant and lurching up the embankment.

Carter fired a burst just as he hit the top, and heard a howl of pain. The man was hit but kept on going.

Carter followed him, staying low. At the top he saw that his quarry had already tumbled down the other side. Now he was limping toward a stand of scrub trees, dragging his right leg.

Carter followed him, firing at the man's legs as he ran.

There was another scream of pain. The man stopped and whirled. A torrent of slugs erupted from the muzzle of his gun. But he was unable to sight, and the slugs went wild. The magnum clicked on empty as the man lost his footing and went down.

Carter approached him quickly but alertly. He had already experienced the suicidal style of Koulami's people. As long as this man was breathing, he was dangerous.

He was lying on his side with one hand slipped inside his jacket over his chest. A dark stain covered his wrist and the exposed area of his shirt. The magnum lay where it had fallen a few paces away.

The man's dark eyes looked steadily up as Carter drew near him.

"Where is Koulami?"

"Fuck you." It was only a whisper, and there was a faint smile on his lips through the blood.

"You're dying, bleeding to death. You could be saved if I got you to a hospital."

Carter took another step and the man's hand whipped away from his chest. In it was a small automatic. He was aiming at Carter's gut and his finger was already squeezing the trigger when the Killmaster's foot swung forward and kicked the gun from his hand.

Carter squeezed off a burst.

The machine gun spit fire and the body leaped convulsively as the slugs thudded into it.

Quickly the echo of the gunfire faded. Far in the distance, from the direction of Alexandria, Carter heard the steady droning throb of police sirens.

Quickly, he grabbed the man's ankles and dragged him back to the road. He gathered the artillery and arranged it around the three bodies.

The Citroen was spewing steam from its radiator, but it was still chugging. Carter's Cortina lay on its side. He backed the Citroen around until he could hook bumpers with the Cortina.

It took three tries, but finally, with an agonized shriek of metal, the little car was righted.

Carter made sure the Cortina was running before he jammed the accelerator on the Citroen and sent it over the cliff.

The sound of the big car crashing into the ocean had barely faded before Carter was in the Cortina speeding on toward the beach.

"Let them figure that one out," he chuckled.

In the center of Maamura village he took an inland road toward the drab suburbs and the desert. He had gone nearly a mile before he found what he wanted.

It was on a side road about a hundred yards off. He stopped at the gate and killed his lights.

Beyond the gate he could see the rusting hulks of at least a hundred cars. He had rented the Cortina for a week, with the proviso of a few more days. When the time came he would report it stolen.

In the meantime, no one would recognize it or spot it in the middle of all these wrecks.

The padlock on the gate took seconds. When the Cortina was buried in the center of the other wrecks, Carter threw the keys as far as he could. He relocked the gate and started jogging cross-country toward the center of the village.

Twenty minutes later he was rousing a cabdriver from his front seat snooze.

"I need to go up the coast to Fawzi Quadima's villa, The Winds. Do you know it?"

"I know it," the driver replied, narrowing one eye at Carter's appearance.

"Had a bit of trouble in a bar, got stranded. You know how it is when you drink too much."

The driver was skeptical, but a wad of money convinced him. A little more money reminded him that he had an uncle who owned a clothing store in the village. For the right price he was sure his uncle would open his shop, even though it was the middle of the night.

He was right.

Carter chose a dark pinstripe as close as he could find to his ruined suit, and a fresh shirt. The tie was usable, and a quick brush took care of the shoes.

An hour later, Carter stepped from the cab and pressed a few more pounds into the driver's hand.

"I wouldn't want to embarrass Mr. Quadima by having the villagers gossip about one of his guests being in a bar brawl . . ."

"Of course," the cabbie said, counting the money with a broad grin. "My lips are sealed."

"I figured they would be."

Carter watched the cab until it was out of sight, and then walked the short distance to the gate. The security guard recognized him but still checked his identification.

Halfway up the graveled lane to the villa, Mohamed

Najjar stepped from the shadows of a tree.

"Don't you ever sleep?" Carter drawled.

"I catnap in the daytime. You had a good evening in Alexandria?"

"Eventful," the Killmaster replied drily, lighting a cigarette.

"Anything I should know about?"

Carter shrugged. "Not that I can think of. The girls at the Mockdar are as ugly as ever, the drinks are more water than whiskey at the Aladdin, and I don't know any more about Koulami than I did this morning."

"I noticed you returned in a taxi."

"I turned my car in. I didn't think I'd be needing it anymore."

At the door, Najjar passed him an envelope. "One of my men took this call for you about an hour ago. I think it is one of your British comrades."

"Thanks."

Carter moved through the house to the seclusion of Quadima's library. Eliza had already told him that the library telephone was the only one in the house that wasn't connected to extensions.

He built a scotch over scotch and dialed.

Effredge answered on the first ring. "Where the hell have you been?"

"I ran into a slight problem. You'll probably read about it in the morning papers. What's up?"

"Your man, Djabi. He's left messages for you all evening. Wouldn't talk to me. Wants you to call no matter what time it is."

"Will do. Anything else?"

"That's it."

"See you in the morning."

Carter broke the connection and dialed Abu Djabi's private number. A husky, irritated voice answered in Arabic.

"This is Carter. Abu called me."

"One moment."

It was only a few seconds until Carter heard the familiar wheeze. "You keep very late hours, my friend."

"I think everybody in Egypt does. You called several times."

"A friend in the police called me earlier this evening. He keeps me informed nightly on the happenings."

"And?"

"The croupier, Hashan, was found in the desert just after sundown. He had a large-caliber bullet in the back of his head."

Carter gritted his teeth. "I fingered him when we met."

"You can't be sure of that, but it is possible."

"Damn," Carter rasped. "They must have followed me and the woman, and then tailed me to the Mockdar."

"Anything is possible. What is important now is that this Koulami knows you are alive and in Egypt. I would move carefully and in the shadows."

"I will."

"In the meantime, I have put more pressure on my people and upped your reward. I assume that is all right?"

"Fine," Carter replied. "Cost is no object."

"I assumed so."

"Did Hashan have a woman?"

"A wife, a shrew, no children. I will take care of her. Do not fret, my friend. Hashan knew the danger. He was a mercenary. When you stop and think about it, we are all mercenaries at heart. We love it or we wouldn't do it."

"I will check in with you tomorrow . . . often."

"Please do. Good night."

Carter grabbed a bottle from the bar and went up to his room. He was nearly stripped when the room-to-room light lit on his phone and buzzed.

"Yes?"

"It's me. I heard you sneak by my room."

"I didn't sneak. I slithered."

"You're a bastard. Dinner was deadly. I hope you had a lousy night."

Carter bit his lip to keep from barking at her. "I had a shitty night and it's almost dawn. I'll see you at breakfast."

"Leave your door unlocked."

"I've got a splitting headache." He hung up before Eliza could reply, and trailed clothes all the way to the bathroom.

He took a quick shower and turned off the lights. He started for the bed, and then remembered. "Well, what the hell," he said to himself, and crossed to the door.

He unlocked it, cursing her style but feeling a little tug in his groin at the same time.

He unwrapped the towel, tossed it over the back of a chair, and got into bed. Some moonlight seeped through the window. The shower had refreshed him. His body didn't feel so tired anymore. But he knew he needed a good night's sleep. He put a sheet over his body and then after a few minutes kicked it down to the foot of the bed with his heels. It was too hot for any kind of covering.

He was sweating. He closed his eyes and was ready to drop off, when the door opened. He kept his eyes closed. Maybe she would go away if she thought he was asleep.

He felt her body on the bed and then soft flesh was against him. A hand passed over his chest. He kept his breathing even. The hand made circles in the thick mat of hair covering his chest.

"You're tense."

"And tired," he replied.

"But not too tired?"

"Eliza . . ."

"Yes?"

The light, cloying quality in her voice grated across his mood, making it worse. "When are you going to realize that this isn't a game served up for your amusement?"

"I'm sure it isn't," she replied. "I know these people are dangerous. And you're dangerous. That's what makes it exciting."

He'd had it.

"Eliza, three of Koulami's people tried to kill me tonight."

Her hand stopped moving. "You're all right?"

"I'm fine, but they're not."

"What happened?" A touch, just a touch, of the fear he had heard when he had first told her about Koulami edged back into her voice.

"I killed them, Eliza. I shot them, one by one."

Her body tensed against him, then drew away. After about five minutes of silence, she slid from the bed and left the room.

Carter turned on his side and went immediately to sleep, with Djabi's words flowing like a slow stream through his mind:

"*. . . we love it or we wouldn't do it.*"

ELEVEN

It was nine o'clock, and the final meeting was scheduled to start in an hour. Quadima himself, his wife, and the personal members of his entourage had arrived by helicopter a half hour before. Inside the villa, the scientific VIPs were finishing their morning meal.

Carter and Harlan Effredge sat at a secluded poolside patio table. Across the pool, the Killmaster saw Eliza Brussman order her third Bloody Mary from one of the passing servants.

They had run into each other twice that morning, and Eliza hadn't spoken to him either time.

Carter reasoned that it was just as well. Now she knew what he was there to do, and she had living—or, in this case, dead—proof that both he and Koulami were for real.

The morning edition of the Alexandria paper had carried the story of the coast road massacre on page one. It was complete with pictures that left little to the imagination.

As yet, the local police had no line on who the victims

were or just who had killed whom. As Carter had suspected, none of the men had had a shred of identification on him.

One possible advantage might come from the previous night's fracus. It was pretty obvious that Koulami had an ego as big as all outdoors. He and his people had missed Carter twice now. The Killmaster was fairly sure the little Iranian terrorist would now score killing him right up there with kidnapping Brussman.

"Nick, are you listening?"

"Sorry, Harlan, my mind is going ninety miles an hour."

"I think we've struck out. I think Koulami has reasoned that Brussman is too tough a nut to crack. He'll pick up his marbles and go home."

"Then what? They need Brussman, or someone like him, to put their toys together."

Effredge shrugged. "That's just it. The Home Office thinks we ought to drop Brussman and go after the toys before they can get them into Iran."

Carter exhaled a cloud of smoke and sighed. "How do we know that they haven't already done that?"

Effredge's face flushed and his shoulders sagged. "We don't."

Carter looked across the table at Eliza and caught her staring at him. Their eyes met, held for a moment, and she looked away.

Carter sucked on his cigarette and watched the cluster of important people milling in the large room behind the villa's glass doors.

As he watched, one of the doors leading from the patio into the villa's great room opened. Mohamed Najjar, flanked by two of his men, stepped out. Najjar's face as he made his way to their table was calm, but his right hand nervously worried a cigarette holder.

"I have relayed your request to Quadima," he said, his lips curling into the first smile Carter had seen since meeting the man.

"And?"

"He has agreed. He and his party, along with Professor Brussman, will leave this afternoon aboard the *Darvais Pride*."

Carter sighed with relief. "What about Peter Donahue and Miss Brussman?"

"The lady has agreed to take the Rome flight this evening. I haven't talked to Mr. Donahue, but I assume he will agree as well."

Carter nodded. "That takes it off both our backs then, doesn't it?"

"Let's hope so," Najjar said. "I will speak to Mr. Donahue the moment he returns."

"Returns?" Carter said. "From where?"

"He did not come back from Alexandria last night."

Carter's eyes whipped around to Eliza Brussman. She was headed around the corner of the pool toward the gardens.

"I'll be back in a second."

He caught her halfway down the steps.

"Where's Donahue?"

"I don't really know. Somewhere in Alexandria, I presume, pursuing his carnal desires."

"He told you where he was going?"

She nodded. "Last evening. He was going to meet a woman . . . a married woman."

"Where?"

"At the casino, I think. Is something wrong?"

"I hope not."

Carter made a beeline for the villa's library and the

telephone. Two minutes later he had Abu Djabi on the horn.

"A bit of luck, perhaps. I just got word. A beggar thinks he may have spotted the woman getting in a car in the Ranji district. He remembers her because few women are dressed so well in that area."

"Did he have an address?"

"Number Seventeen, Al Haran Street."

"Inform the beggar he can retire if his information is accurate."

Djabi chuckled. "I already have. Good luck, my friend."

Najjar was still talking to Effredge at the table. Now that the party was almost over, the two men had set aside many of their differences.

Carter broke in with a fast explanation.

"I can have an antiterrorist team there in less than an hour," Najjar said.

"Then let's move!" Carter said, already heading toward the parking area.

The meeting took place in a gray building in the midst of one of Cairo's worst slums. It was one building of dingy apartments in a block of many. The facade of the building was molded plaster, chipped in most places, peeling in others. Garbage was piled in front of it and in an adjoining alley.

The single room of the sixth-floor apartment was devoid of furniture other than a single scarred table and a few chairs.

At one end of the table sat Amin Koulami, flanked by two of his best men.

At the other end sat Saiad Muchasi. He had brought two of his people.

Between them, on the table, was a briefcase stuffed with Egyptian pound notes.

Muchasi was a large, square-shouldered, square-jawed man with a deeply windburned face. His age was impossible to determine beneath several days' worth of stubble. When he spoke, which was rare, it was usually in grunts.

For the last two years Saiad Muchasi had been head of the People's Front for Freedom. He had coined the name himself to give political legitimacy to killing, kidnapping, robbery, and any other crime that would secure a profit.

Like many adventuresome thieves the world over, Muchasi had embraced politics and terrorism as a way to line his pockets and enrich those around him.

It was Muchasi's nomadic cousins who had smuggled the plutonium and nuclear fuel across the Saudi deserts and into Bahrain. Now he was being paid for performing the second part of the bargain he had struck with Koulami months before.

"The man, Donahue, is still drugged?"

"Yes," Koulami replied, "in the flat below. The ransom demand will be delivered to the villa early this evening."

"You are too good to me, Amin Koulami. You pay me to carry on a kidnapping that you have already done. Then you show me the way to collect the ransom for myself from this Donahue."

Koulami shrugged. "Your cousins have transported our goods with faith. You supply us with the boat we need at Fa'id. I am merely completing your payment with British money."

Muchasi leaned forward, grinning through his dark beard. "Amin Koulami is a shrewd man. I think he gives nothing for nothing.''

Koulami matched the other man's grin. "I have told you what I want. You are not to negotiate fully for at least seventy-two hours. When the exchange is made at last, hand over Donahue. But kill the agent, Carter. I ask no more than that.''

Muchasi looked to his two cohorts and saw his own greed reflected in their eyes.

"Done, Amin Koulami. A bargain.''

Koulami stood and walked from the room. Halfway down the stairs, Achmed spoke.

"He and his entire tribe are no match for MI6 and Carter.''

"I am well aware of that,'' Koulami said, a sly smile stretching his lips. "But they will buy us what we most need, time. And if one of them kills Carter, it will just be a plus.''

Najjar's team was good. They evacuated the houses on both sides of Number 17 quickly, quietly, and efficiently.

When the time came they went in as a unit, covering all the exits and the roofs.

Effredge and Carter were relegated to a Mercedes sedan a block from the site. Silently, they smoked and waited and watched.

Between them on the seat, an open walkie-talkie let them know the progress.

"Ready on the roofs?''

"Ready.''

"Unit Two is inside the cellar.''

"This is Unit Three. We're over the wall and in the courtyard. No signs of activity.''

"Unit One?''

"Ready at the front."

"Go!"

They heard the exploding pop of a grenade launcher and saw windows all along the front of the house shatter. In seconds, tear gas flooded through the broken windows into the street. Then they saw the first team hit the front door.

"Unit One. We're inside."

"Unit Two. Something strange about the cellar door we're checking."

"Control, this is Unit One. There's a high-wire and a trip-wire in the main hall."

"All units," Najjar's voice barked, "the whole house is booby-trapped! Back off for the second team!"

Carter saw the bomb squad leave their van and enter the house. He flipped his cigarette out the window and glanced over at Effredge.

"They've flown."

"Looks that way," the MI6 man replied.

Ten minutes later, Najjar approached the car.

"They're gone. There is no doubt that they were in there, but there's no sign of them now."

"Anybody hurt?" Carter asked.

"No, we spotted the booby traps in time. I'll have a forensics team go over the place, and my people will interrogate the neighborhood."

"The interrogation might do some good," Carter replied. "But the house will be clean."

"Probably."

"Mind if we take the car back to the villa? I want to check the *Darvais Pride* by radio, and I'd like to take Miss Brussman to the airport myself."

"Of course, go ahead. I'll follow as soon as everybody's working."

The powerful motor of the Mercedes purred to life. Carter made a U-turn and headed for the coast road.

"He's beat us again," Effredge said.

"Yeah," Carter growled. "The bastard moves like a cobra."

Carter finished the light meal a servant had brought to his room, and pushed the plate away. He lit a cigarette and wandered to the window. Below, the pool shimmered in the floodlights. At the bottom of the hill, two of Najjar's men lounged against the tall wrought-iron gate and smoked.

Their job would soon be over. He had checked the *Darvais Pride*. She was under full power and about an hour from Port Said. At the speed she was moving, she would be through the canal and well down the Red Sea by morning.

It was nearly eight o'clock. Eliza's plane left at nine-thirty. It was time to collect her. He shrugged into Wilhelmina's shoulder rig and was reaching for his coat when the door opened.

Eliza stood trancelike in the doorway. Her eyes were glassy and her face was deathly pale.

"Eliza, what the hell . . ."

She thrust an envelope and a single sheet of paper into Carter's hand.

"The cook just gave me this. She was shopping in the village. When she returned she found it in one of her baskets. Since it had my name on the envelope, she brought it right to me."

Carter flipped the sheet of paper and scanned it. It was a message made up of cut-out newspaper letters:

WE HAVE PETER DONAHUE. TELL THE AMERICAN CARTER BUT NO ONE ELSE. IF THE

EGYPTIAN AUTHORITIES ARE TOLD WE KILL HIM AT ONCE. STAND BY TELEPHONE EIGHT A.M.

"Nick, what do they want?" Eliza cried. "Peter knows nothing. He—"

"He doesn't have to know anything. If it's Koulami, he wants us . . . you and me."

"Us? My God, what for?"

"Me, for my skin. You . . . to get at your father."

Her skin turned even paler. "What are we going to do?"

"The only thing we can do. Wait until eight o'clock in the morning. C'mon in, I'll fix you a drink. You look like you need one."

The bottle of scotch was three quarters of the way down and Carter didn't feel better. Eliza had done her share of hitting, and he could tell, even from across the room, that the booze was having very little effect on her as well.

In the last two hours he had left the room once, to check again on the progress of the *Darvais Pride*. Everything okay there.

"Do you want to get some sleep?" he had asked.

"No. May I have another drink?"

"Sure."

Neither had spoken of taking her to the airport. Leaving had been out of the question for her, and Carter hadn't pushed.

Now he lounged on the big sofa while she sat by the window, absorbed in her own thoughts, now and then throwing out a comment.

"Now I'm really scared."

"You should be."

"You're right," she said, pausing to sip from her glass. "I've been an ass."

Carter didn't answer that one.

"Peter is a nice boy. He doesn't deserve to be involved in this. Will they harm him?"

"They might," Carter said, "if we don't follow instructions until we see a way to spring him. My hunch is they want to get you and me close. They don't really care about Donahue."

She turned. The light was behind her, and he couldn't see her face. "So you'll try to rescue him?"

"I will rescue him. The rub is, I won't risk you to do it."

"What if I'm part of the deal?"

"Then they can go to hell."

"Rather than risk me, you'd let them kill Peter?" she gasped.

Carter killed time by stubbing out his cigarette. "Yeah, I would."

"At least you're truthful."

"They can get to your father through you. They can't through Peter. It's as simple as that."

"It's a shitty deal."

"Yeah, it sure as hell is. But they're shitty people."

She finished her drink and set the glass aside. "You're a hard bastard, you know that? But I guess people like you have to be."

Carter didn't answer that one either.

Then she was moving toward him, her hips swaying sensuously in the tight skirt where it hugged her body. As she stopped in front of him, her hand went to the buttons on her blouse.

"I'm sorry about last night. I was an ass."

"Do you know what you're doing, Eliza?"

"No, but please don't try to tell me."

She leaned over to kiss him. Her parted lips drew him to her. At contact, her lips parted further. She drew his tongue into her mouth and caressed it with hers.

When she stood again, she slowly unbuttoned the blouse and let it fall free. Then she was twisting her hips, easing the slim skirt over her thighs.

Carter stared at her face instead of her voluptuous figure.

"Why?" he asked. "Curiosity about someone who kills people for a living?"

"Perhaps. Maybe I don't think you're any different, really, than they are."

The laugh that rolled from Carter's throat was hollow.

"Or maybe it's to prove to you that you're missing something," she murmured.

"Or prove to you that I'm man enough to let them kill Donahue."

"I don't know," she growled low in her throat. "Let's find out."

He took hold of her hair and pulled her head back. "Just because I kill people, Eliza, doesn't mean I'm a man," and he laughed and let her fall on top of him.

She was picking at the buttons of his shirt, fastening her mouth to his chest. When she finally had him naked to the waist, she slipped off the rest of her own clothes and pressed his face into her breasts. They were smothering him.

She had to work his hands for him, run them along her legs. Her lips were sucking at his ribs as if to draw blood.

Then she was above him, straddling his body.

Carter gave up and let the room start to swim.

When it was over and she was back at the window, he lit a cigarette.

"Well?" he said at last.

"Not much," she replied without turning. "You still think I'm a spoiled brat who takes nothing seriously?"

"Yes, I do. And I still think you're an ass, as well."

She turned and walked back to the sofa to stare down at him. "Then you should know that it's through Peter that they can get to my father. Believe me, Carter, Josef Brussman could care less what happens to his daughter. But he would go to the gates of hell to save his son."

·

TWELVE

The sun was just coming up when Captain Denton Jurgens strolled along the deck, morning coffee in hand, toward the wheelhouse.

Jurgens had retired eight years previously from the Royal Navy. He had served since in Oman and Bahrain as a naval advisor. It was in Bahrain that he had caught the eye of Fawzi Quadima and been offered his present position.

He had jumped at it. His job as skipper of the *Darvais Pride* was the least taxing of any position he had had thus far in life, and he was looking forward to living out his days in luxurious retirement as master of what had become, in all but name, his very own floating palace.

In the next two hours, Captain Denton Jurgens would rue the day he took over the *Darvais Pride*.

He mounted the steps to the wheelhouse and nodded to his first officer. "Good morning, Mr. Miller."

"Good morning, sir."

"Something wrong, son?"

"I don't know, sir. There's a large ketch there, sir.

She's under both power and sail, and she's been running parallel to us for the last hour.''

"Where?" Jurgens set his cup aside and lifted a pair of field glasses from his chest.

"There, to starboard, sir, about a half mile. She seems to be closing on us."

She was a thirty-footer, two-masted and sleek. Jurgens could see exhaust coming from both her stern pipes, and she was riding every inch of sail she had aboard.

"Odd, that, under full sail with her power on."

"I agree, sir. I've been pacing her, and she puts on a knot or two when we speed up. She also begins tacking if we throttle back."

"She does seem to be closing a bit. What's our position?"

"Just south of Fa'id, sir. We should be sighting the locks just short of an hour. Should I alert security, sir?"

"No, don't think so, Mr. Miller, not unless they close hard. Go below, get yourself some coffee. I'll keep an eye on her."

"Aye-aye, sir."

As the first officer left the bridge, Jurgens adjusted the powerful glasses to a finer focus.

He counted three men: a deckhand curling line in the stern, a helmsman, and what appeared to be the master. He was directing two young women through the rigging.

Good sailors, Jurgens thought, and damned attractive women. More than likely just out for an early-morning cruise.

Captain Jurgens forgot the ketch and turned to his chart table. With a sigh, he started filling out the many multiple forms that would see them through the canal.

●　　●　　●

Carter heard the whooshing sound of the opening drapes. He opened his eyes, and immediately tried to close them again. They didn't make it.

"Coffee?"

Carter winced as he got Eliza Brussman into focus. She had changed into a white jump suit. He guessed that she had been up all night, but she looked alert and fresh-scrubbed.

"Yeah, coffee."

"You like it black?"

"Yeah, black."

"You fell asleep."

"I know," he said, accepting the cup with a shaky hand. "You?"

"No, I stood under a shower for an hour. Confession must be good for the soul. I feel wonderful."

"Good for you," Carter mumbled.

His eyes felt like mud cracking in the sun. There were little men trying to dig a tunnel through his brain. His mouth felt like it had been sucking on alum all night, and his breath reeked of stale alcohol.

"Would you like a shower?" she asked.

"That would be nice."

He watched her cross the room, and came up to a sitting position very carefully in case his head fell off. He sipped some coffee, felt it burn his tongue, and sipped some more.

She came back into sight. "Shower's running."

"I can hear it. What time is it?"

"Six-thirty. Your MI6 friends are downstairs. Don't drown. I'll be back."

Carter got to his feet, and only then did he realize that he was stark naked.

And then he remembered.

She had talked about herself, her father, and Peter Donahue for nearly an hour. At the end of it, Carter had carried her to the bed and they had made love a second time.

Only the second time was far different—and far more satisfying—for both of them.

As he stepped under the spray, the trials and tribulations of the family Brussman came back to him in a rush.

According to Eliza, she had never been bounced on her daddy's knee. In fact, from her first childhood memories, she couldn't remember a kind word or a warm glance from her father.

Her mother was the daughter of a peer who promptly disinherited her for marrying out of her class. Brussman was a Jew, and, worse yet, a poor Jew, the son of a German refugee.

In time, probably after Eliza's birth, the strain got to both her parents. Her mother had given up everything, the life she knew, for a man who didn't love her. Slowly she had begun to realize that Josef Brussman had married her for only two reasons: his ego, and a son.

In the end, the bolstering of his ego became meaningless, and she had birthed a daughter instead of a son.

Brussman ignored his wife and daughter beyond providing for their welfare. He sought out women for affairs with the same tenacity with which he pursued success and wealth.

Finally he settled on one woman. Her name was Patricia Donahue. Probably the strongest reason for this was the fact that she bore him a male child. Of course, because of the prestige of his position, Brussman couldn't openly declare that Peter was his son. But that didn't stop him from grooming the young man, providing his education, and, when the time was right, hiring him so that he could keep his offspring close to him.

"Does Peter know?" Carter had asked when she had finished her story.

"No."

Brussman's mistress and his wife died within a year of each other. But before her mother died, she told Eliza the whole tale. The girl had grown up blackmailing her father. In return for her silence, Eliza was given the same good life and privileges as her half brother.

"So you see, Nick, that whoever these people are, it is just luck that they have kidnapped the right person. If it were me, he would never accede to their demands. But Peter is a different story."

So, Carter thought, stepping from the shower and reaching for a towel, *Peter has to be returned before Brussman learns he has been taken*.

He managed to shave, dress, and get down another cup of coffee. By the time he had joined Effredge and the others, he felt alive again.

It was seven-thirty.

"Captain, that ketch looks like she's cutting right across our bow!"

Jurgens's head jerked up at the helmsman's words. "Damned fools. Throttle back, half speed!"

"Aye-aye, sir."

The bow dipped as the powerful twin diesels in her bowels slowed. Jurgens put the binoculars to his eyes and raked the deck of the ketch.

Sure enough, the ketch's skipper was directing his craft right into the path of the *Darvais Pride*.

"What the hell are they up to, sir?"

"Damned if I know, but I'm going to find out. Cut your speed back to a quarter, and prepare to stop engines if that fool doesn't change course."

"Aye, sir."

Jurgens grabbed a bull horn and headed for the bow. The head of Quadima's security force had also seen the ketch. He fell in step beside the captain.

"What's going on?"

"Probably carelessness. We'll find out soon enough."

The two other security men joined them, their machine pistols at the ready.

By the time they reached the bow, the smaller boat had heeled over slightly and was running parallel to the *Darvais Pride*, not more than a dangerous thirty yards to starboard.

"Ahoy, the ketch! Do you speak English?"

The small dapper man with the thin mustache that Jurgens had already guessed was the ketch's captain stepped to the rail. He, too, had a bull horn.

"Most assuredly, Captain Jurgens. We all speak English quite fluently."

"Just what the hell do you think you're doing?" Jurgens replied, and then he realized that the man had addressed him by name. "You know my name?"

"I do, Captain, as well as the name of every person on the *Darvais Pride*."

"It's a hijack," the security chief growled, and raised his machine pistol. His comrades did the same.

"Wait," Jurgens barked. "I don't see any arms."

"Captain?" came the call from the other vessel.

"Yes?"

"This, Captain, is a radio control device." He held up a small black box about the size of a cigarette carton.

"As you can see, one of the young ladies in the bow has another just like it. Selwa?"

"Yes."

"Go ahead!"

As Jurgens and the others watched, one of the two women spun the prop of a model airplane. Its miniature engine roared to life and, controlled by the box in the other woman's hand, it sailed out over the water.

"Damned practical joke of some kind," Jurgens roared, and turned back to the wheelhouse. "Helmsman!"

"Aye, sir."

"Full speed ahead!"

"With all due respect, I wouldn't do that, Captain. Keep your eye on the airplane."

The little craft did a couple of loops, barreled, and sailed back toward the yacht. When it was directly overhead about a hundred feet up, there was a powerful explosion.

The men on the *Darvais Pride* all ducked to avoid the falling debris.

Jurgens whirled to the little man on the opposite deck. "What the hell do you think you're doing!" he yelled.

"Captain, there are eight bombs planted against the hull of the *Darvais Pride*. Any one of seven of them could blow you in half."

The little man paused, going so far as to calmly light a cigarette while he let that sink in. Then he spoke again.

"I want your security people to place their guns on the deck and step away from them. I want you to stop engines, and I want you—"

"You can go to hell!" Jurgens roared.

The other man flipped one of the buttons on the box

in his hand. There was a muffled explosion from just under the yacht's bow, and a geyser of water soared into the air.

"That was just proof that the bombs are there, Captain. Now do as you're told."

Jurgens's face went gray and his fists clenched. "Get Quadima."

The security chief ran to the hatch, and moments later appeared with Quadima himself.

"What is going on, Captain?"

In sputtered, staccato words, Jurgens explained. Quadima's wise, dark eyes didn't blink. When Jurgens finished, he turned to the ketch.

"What do you want?"

"Surely it must be obvious. I'm hijacking the *Darvais Pride* and everyone on it."

"Do you want money?"

The little man cackled with laughter. "Money? I have no use for money. You have one minute."

Quadima had never been an emotional man and he wasn't one now. Quietly and rationally, he weighed the circumstances and realized that they were outmaneuvered.

The minute was almost up when he turned to Jurgens. "Do as they say."

The engines were stopped and the ketch pulled alongside, close enough to toss grappling hooks.

Two more men appeared on the deck of the ketch. As the little man with the mustache climbed over the rail of the *Darvais Pride*, the men behind him attached a tarpaulin on the stern decks.

"Good morning, Captain. Your Excellency. I am Amin Koulami."

"The terrorist," Quadima said hollowly.

"Not at all . . . the revolutionary. I know that you are checking in by radio with Egyptian security until you are through the canal and have cleared Egyptian waters in the Red Sea. What time is your next communication due, Captain?"

Captain Jurgens looked to the ship's owner. Quadima's dark eyes were smoldering and his lips were a thin line beneath his beard. At last he nodded.

"Just about now . . . two or three minutes."

Koulami nodded. "You will make the usual transmission and report no trouble. One of my people will, of course, monitor you even though it is not necessary. Should you deviate from your usual report and alert the authorities, you would be committing suicide. If an Egyptian gunboat even approaches us, I assure you I will blow us all to hell. Selwa!"

"Yes, Amin?"

"Accompany the captain."

"Yes, Amin."

The two of them moved aft toward the wheelhouse.

By now several crates had been transferred to the deck of the yacht and were already being covered by the tarp and tied down. The ketch, with just two men aboard, had cast free of the yacht and was already moving away.

"You will list these crates as personal property on the canal manifests, Your Excellency," Koulami said. "With your prestige, I am sure there will be no inspection."

By now all the others aboard had come up on the main deck. Koulami's eyes roved over their faces and fell on Josef Brussman.

"If it isn't money," Quadima said, "just what do you want?"

"Safe passage of my goods through the canal, Your Excellency."

"What for?"

"I'm sure Dr. Brussman can answer that, can't you?"

Brussman cleared his throat. "They have plutonium and nuclear fuel in the crates. They want me to build them a bomb and a reactor."

Quadima cursed an astonished oath in Arabic.

Koulami glanced briefly at each of the men. "As long as Dr. Brussman does as he is told, none of you has anything to fear."

Brussman stepped forward, his eyes on a direct level with the little terrorist. "Go to hell."

Koulami didn't speak. He turned and walked to the edge of the bow. He stooped and picked up one of the machine pistols. It was barely in his hands before he turned and fired.

Ten slugs ripped into the body of one of Quadima's men, driving him over the rail and into the sea.

"I think you will do as I say, Dr. Brussman, or the blood of everyone aboard the *Darvais Pride* will be on your hands."

Harlan Effredge and Eliza were waiting in the library. On the table between them was a plate of sweet rolls, a large pot of coffee, and the telephone.

"We goofed," Effredge said. "She's told me about Donahue."

Carter shrugged as he poured a fresh cup. "We didn't know. Has the *Darvais Pride* checked in?"

"About five minutes ago. Everything is all right there. Should we bring in Najjar?"

"We might have to, but let's wait until they declare some terms."

They killed time smoking, drinking coffee, and avoiding one another's eyes. When the telephone rang, Carter grabbed it.

"Yes."

"To whom am I speaking?" The English was heavily accented and the voice was a growling rasp.

"Carter."

"Good morning, Carter. First of all, Peter Donahue is alive and quite safe."

"What do you want for him?"

"That will be determined in the next two days."

"Two days," Carter hissed. "You're mad. Why wait two days?"

"It is not your place to question our motives, Carter. Stay by the telephone. We will contact you at eight each morning and eight each evening . . ."

"Wait."

"Yes?"

"Whatever you want in return for Donahue will take time to prepare. Can you give me some hint?"

There was a pause on the other end of the line and a muted conversation in Arabic. Finally the voice came back: "I have instructions not to negotiate for seventy-two hours. But I will tell you this: the safe return of Peter Donahue will require money . . . a very, very great deal of money."

Carter's eyes widened in surprise. "Money?"

"That is correct, Carter, money. Lots of money. And let me caution you again: do not alert Egyptian security. If we have any hint that you have, Peter Donahue is dead."

The line went dead and Carter slowly replaced the receiver.

"What is it?" Eliza asked. "What do they want?"

"Money," Carter replied.

"*Money?*" Effredge declared. "No mention of Brussman?"

"None, and they won't get down to it for seventy-two hours."

"It's crazy, a diversion of some kind."

"Maybe," Carter said, "but this changes the picture if it's true. Eliza . . ."

"Yes?"

"This family secret business, about Peter . . ."

"Yes?"

"We've assumed Koulami found out about Peter somehow. That's why he was taken instead of you."

"Yes."

"Yet you've said many times that no one outside of you and your father knew. How sure are you of that?"

She leaned her head on her hands in thought and took a great deal of time answering. At last she rolled her eyes up to Carter. "Now that I think of it, there's no conceivable way anyone else could have known. Both my mother and Patricia Donahue did exactly as my father wished. Peter was born in a small, private hospital outside of Paris. There was nothing to attach Peter or his mother to any of us."

Carter pushed a legal pad toward her and handed her a pen. "I want dates, names, places, Eliza. Every detail you can think of concerning all of you."

As she began to write, Carter and Effredge moved across the room.

"Octopus?" Effredge said.

Carter nodded.

Octopus was the master computer at Langley. If anyone in the Western world had a security clearance, their background information had at one time or another been fed into it.

"If Octopus doesn't know the real story behind Peter Donahue, then it's a pretty sure thing Koulami wouldn't know."

"The seventy-two hours," Effredge said. "It is a diversion."

"Looks that way," Carter said. "Step up the checks on the *Darvais Pride*. It looks like Koulami means to draw us away and hit it. Also, get Najjar in here. I don't care what they say; we're going to need official help on this now."

Effredge left the room. Eliza continued to write furiously as she recalled details.

Carter got back on the phone. It was time to let the old thief, Abu Djabi, in on the whole action. His army of thieves and informants might still prove to be the one difference in the whole mess.

THIRTEEN

Time.

They say the Swiss measure it, the French hoard it, the Italians squander it, and the Americans profit from it.

Well, right now, time was on the side of Koulami: time, and the element of surprise. Obviously the little terrorist was buying it with Peter Donahue. But only with distraction in mind.

Octopus had come back with a complete printout. Nothing in it even hinted that Peter Donahue was the son of Dr. Josef Brussman. It wasn't a long shot for Carter to surmise that Koulami was just trying to muddy the waters. The man had no idea that he had kidnapped the key to Josef Brussman.

The evening phone call was no more than a check-in. Carter hadn't pushed the question beyond trying to get a dollar figure. The caller was vague but again stressed a "large amount."

Najjar had jumped in with both feet. Surprisingly, he now gave Effredge and the Killmaster his fullest cooperation.

He had his people combing everywhere and coordinating with the street people of Abu Djabi.

A mountain of electronic equipment was brought in for the evening call. Carter kept the contact as long as possible, but it wasn't long enough to get a definite trace.

"Sorry," Najjar said, reporting from his operators. "All we could get is an area."

"Where?"

"It's a Cairo exchange."

"Can you rig a ring-through from this phone to your Cairo headquarters? I want to be close to them for the next call in the morning."

"I'll have my people get right on it."

"Good enough," Carter said, turning to Eliza. "I'll get you on the early-morning flight from Cairo to Rome."

"No."

"Yes."

"Nick, all this isn't Peter's fault. He's being used and he has no idea why. I've never been able to openly call him 'brother,' but he *is* my brother. In many ways, my father has hurt him as much as me. I want to see this through."

Carter was about to object again, but he saw that it would be useless.

"Okay, but you stick to me like glue. This could still be a ruse to get at you."

Najjar provided a car and a driver. Effredge and his people would drive two other cars, a lead and a backup, in caravan. Also, MI6 had a safe house that even the Egyptians didn't know about. It was there that Carter and Eliza would spend the night.

An hour later they were headed south on the road to Cairo.

It was almost two in the morning when they were dropped off in front of the safe house. It was in the wealthy Rajadi section of the city. Three of Najjar's boys would patrol the grounds all night.

Only a section of the house had been maintained, three rooms on the second floor. One of them served as a kitchen, another as a study/office with a single desk, chair, and telephone.

"There's only one bedroom."

Eliza smiled a crooked smile and rolled her eyes. "Good God, Carter, you think that makes any difference now?"

"No," he grinned sheepishly, "I guess not."

She headed toward the bathroom with bag in hand. Carter scared up a bottle and a couple of glasses.

He wasn't too sure he was going to be able to sleep anyhow.

He rummaged through the kitchen until he had the semblance of a meal. It was ready by the time she emerged from the bath.

"Hungry?"

"Not really." She poured a little whiskey into a glass and added water from a bottle.

She wore the same nearly transparent negligee she had worn when she slipped into his room at the villa. But over it now was a layered peignoir that demurely concealed her body.

"You're sure?" he asked, building himself a sandwich.

"I'm sure." She sipped her drink and stared at him as he ate. "Nick?"

"Yeah?"

"Coming down in the car, you said that you were going to push them. What did you mean?"

He chewed, swallowed, and washed it down with scotch. When he spoke at last, he chose his words carefully.

"I'm gambling that it's not Koulami who has Peter."

"Then who?"

"There are renegade terrorist groups all over the Middle East. They're not in this for any true cause. It's profit under the guise of terrorism. I'm guessing that Koulami put the snitch on Peter and turned him over to one of these groups."

"But what can he gain?"

"Time, and keeping us occupied while he goes after your father in his own way, whatever that is."

She emptied the glass and set it on the table. "What are you going to do in the morning?"

"Try to push up their timetable . . . confuse them."

"How?" she asked, turning slowly back to face him.

Carter pushed the plate of food away. He had lost his appetite.

"By confusing them. By telling them that Peter isn't worth a *very large* amount of money."

"My God . . ."

"I'm going to try and force them into immediate negotiations . . . tomorrow, if possible."

"But surely you'll pay their ransom if there's any chance . . ."

"Eliza, believe me—if I'm right about Peter's captors, they have no intention of turning Peter over to us even if we pay."

"Then my father should be told! He could force them—"

"No."

"Jesus, you don't care, do you?"

Carter lit a cigarette, letting the smoke mask his features. "It doesn't make any difference if I care."

Like a robot she moved across the room to the tier of bunk beds. Facing away from him, she shed the peignoir and slid beneath the covers in the lower bunk.

"Either way, Eliza," Carter murmured to her back, "we'll have to get Peter back by force. Believe me—"

"I can't believe any of it. Jesus, you are a hard bastard."

Carter smoked in silence, knowing it was futile to explain his plan. She wouldn't understand.

He finished his cigarette, turned out the lamp, and undressed in the darkness. Just as he was about to climb into the upper bunk, he touched her shoulder.

"Good night, Carter."

The ring-through worked perfectly. At a few seconds past eight, the telephone rang.

Carter waited until Najjar's man gave him the sign.

"Yes?"

"Carter?"

"Yes."

"You have done very good so far. Only twenty-four hours and we will meet."

"No."

There was a long silence and the voice, when it returned, was tense. "What do you mean, 'no'?"

"Just that. No. I have consulted with Washington and London, and my people see no reason to carry on with this farce any longer."

"Farce? Just what do you mean by *farce*, Carter?"

"Peter Donahue's value to us is negotiable. The short of it is, he is not worth as much money as you seem to want."

"I think you are bluffing."

"Think what you want. Good-bye."

"Wait!" A short hesitation. "You want him dead?"

"Of course not. He is a British citizen. But without demands, there can be no negotiation. And without negotiation, we see no reason to tie up our people any longer."

"One moment."

Carter looked up at the man on the other phone. The Egyptian held up two fingers for two minutes. One of those minutes dragged by before the caller came back on the line.

"We will call you back in one hour."

The line was dead.

Carter knew before they told him that the trace had been completed.

"Well?"

"We got it, but it won't do any good. It's a call box in the Amali district."

Carter nodded. "They'll just switch to another phone booth next time."

"That's it."

"What do you think?" Effredge asked.

"I think they'll play," Carter replied. "Put your people on alert. I've already told Djabi."

The Killmaster moved down the hall to a small dining room. Eliza, looking tired and haggard, sat drinking tea. She glanced up when he entered.

"Well?"

"They'll call back in an hour. I think they'll take the bait."

"And kill Peter as soon as they have it."

"No, Eliza. I'm more sure now than ever. They want money. They won't kill the goose until the golden egg is laid."

Carter sat with her, trying to answer the questions she asked about the method he planned to use to rescue Donahue. When he left her to return to the communications room, he was pretty sure she felt better: queasy about the method, but better about Peter Donahue's chances for survival.

He entered the computer room just as the ship-to-shore shut down.

"That was the *Darvais Pride*. No sign of anything out of the ordinary. They should be out of the Gulf of Aden by late tonight and heading around Oman by morning."

Carter walked to a huge wall map and traced the route of the *Darvais Pride*. He ran a pointer up the Gulf of Oman and then into the Persian Gulf. The tip of the pointer stopped just off Bahrain.

"Interesting . . ."

"What's that?" Effredge said at his shoulder.

"Keeping approximately the same speed from the time Eliza got the note in the cook's basket, the yacht's location would be here, just off Bahrain, at the end of the seventy-two hours."

"And just across from the coast of Iran."

"Yeah."

"Think that's when Koulami plans to hit?"

"Could be," Carter replied. "Maybe we—"

The hot phone they had set up rang, interrupting both their thoughts and discussion.

"Yes, Carter here."

"We are prepared to deal immediately."

"That's very sensible of you," Carter replied, hearing the audible sighs of relief from the others in the room. "This will only be a preparatory meeting, of course."

"To make sure we understand each other, American, what do *you* mean by 'preparatory'?"

"I'll want to see Peter Donahue, to make sure he is alive and unharmed."

"That is agreed."

"And to negotiate the price and means of trade."

"Agreed, but I tell you now, Carter, we will not negotiate the place for the exchange. That we decide on ourselves. Agreed?"

Carter had already assumed this, but he still took several seconds to answer. "Agreed," he said at last.

"You will have to come to Cairo."

"That will be no problem," Carter said, giving nothing away in his voice that they had already made the move from Alexandria.

"Excellent. Now listen carefully. At precisely noon, take a taxi at the Mosque of Al Axhar. Instruct the driver to take you to Tahrir Square. Walk across the square and get into another taxi. Have this one take you to El Gamhuria Square. On the side of the Palace Museum there is a bank of call boxes. Wait for the second one to ring. Do you understand?"

"I understand."

"One other thing."

"Yes?"

"We want the woman to enter the main dining room of the houseboat *Omar Khayyam*. She will dine there until she receives a call."

"No," Carter said.

"Yes, this is the only way we will deal."

"So if anyone follows me, she is available to take Donahue's place."

"No, Mr. Carter. If anyone follows you, we will shoot the woman. Good day."

Carter dropped the phone. "Shit."

"It's really no problem," Effredge said, "the way you've got it figured."

"No, we can cover her," Carter replied. "I just didn't want to use her unless we had to."

He crossed the room and lifted a second phone. Instantly the connection was made.

"Abu?"

"Yes, my friend."

Quickly he gave the old thief the route.

"It sounds as though they will use a cutout, my friend."

"It would seem so."

"Most likely, you will never reach the phones at the museum."

"That's what I figure," Carter growled. "Do your people have the cameras?"

"Oh, yes, and they have been instructed in their use. I will have them all along the route, have no fear of that."

"Good. And, remember, Abu, no one is to try and follow. Only the pictures."

"My people are as shadows."

Carter replaced the phone. There was already a scurry of activity in the room. He headed back down the hallway to tell Eliza Brussman that she was about to be put on the hot seat with him.

In the sudden surge of the moment, the planning, and the adrenaline running through his body, he had forgotten about the *Darvais Pride* and the timetable of the yacht's arrival in the middle of the Persian Gulf.

FOURTEEN

At precisely noon sharp, Carter stepped from the shade of the Al Axhar Mosque. He ambled among tourists clutching their children and cameras until he reached a long line of taxis.

The one he chose was less than a year old, but it looked as if it had led an attack in the '67 Egypt-Israeli war.

"Where?"

"Tahrir Square," Carter replied, and fought the G-force that sent him into the seat as the driver applied the gas and plowed through the gears.

Like a missile with a faulty guidance system they flew through the streets of Cairo's oldest quarter. On the turns, the driver and his machine defied gravity. On the straightaways, they defied other machines, donkey carts, stray sheep and goats, and a shifting sea of human pedestrians.

Carter could only hope, as they flew through the maze, that in that throng of humanity Abu Djabi's

people were waiting, clicking their cameras at the fol-
low-up car.

They would have to have one somewhere behind him
to make sure that he didn't have a tail.

They passed the Abdin Palace at Opera Square and
hurtled into the wide boulevard Shari' Qasr Al-Nil.
Ahead, Carter could see the tower above the square and
behind it the Nile Hilton.

And then they were in the square, careening through
the traffic circle.

"Where?"

"Here is fine," Carter replied.

The driver took a full inch of rubber off his tires
screaming to a halt. He held his hand, palm up, over the
seat.

He hadn't bothered pulling to the curb, and behind
them a million horns sounded like the mating call of two
million camels.

Carter shoved a wad of bills in his hand and dived
through the door. He barely made the sidewalk with two
motorcycles, a Vespa, and another cab trying to disen-
gage his torso from his legs.

Instead of dodging traffic and other pedestrians—
neither of which paid any attention to lights across the
square—he chose to walk around. He took the higher
elevation of steps the whole way around the square. By
so doing, his watchers would be able to spot him easily.

And, he hoped, Djabi's people would be able to spot
them.

As he moved, his eyes took in everything. And
everywhere he saw people. They thronged the walkway
and the street. They poured from shops and offices and
strolled casually in front of hurtling cars and motorcycles.

At last he reached the opposite side of the square. There were no stands, so he had to take his life in his hands and wade into the street to hail a cab.

His arm had barely reached his shoulder when four stopped. Carter rolled into the rear seat of the closest one, a Mercedes that its German engineers would never admit they designed.

"Where?"

"El Gamhuria Square," Carter said in Arabic, "and double your fare if you go under the speed limit."

The driver shot off Tahrir with a roaring laugh. "In Cairo there are no speed limits!"

"Then keep it under the speed of sound," Carter replied, gripping a handle on each door as they bore down on a thick line of schoolchildren crossing the narrow street in front of them.

The driver leaned on his horn, didn't touch his brakes, and the youthful humanity parted like the sea before the bow of his machine. The rear of the Mercedes had barely cleared when the line closed behind it.

At El Gamhuria, the driver was kind. He not only found the curb, he drove right up on it to discharge his passenger.

Carter thanked him profusely, paid him the promised double fare, and staggered back out into the blistering heat.

He had to go around the square and down three blocks to reach the museum.

They hit him one block short of it. A tiny Opel with two men in it—the driver and a passenger in the rear—cut him off just as he was crossing the mouth of a narrow alley.

The rear door opened and there was a guttural cry. "Get in!"

Carter did.

Both men were swathed from head to toe in white, flowing *galabiyas*, with desert burnooses wound tightly around their faces.

The one in the rear had a monster Webley pointed directly at Carter's gut.

"Do as you're told."

"I was told to go to the call boxes by the—"

"Now you're being told something else. Do as you're told."

The alley was narrow, barely the width of two cars and then only if neither of them were larger than the Opel and both of them rode the curbs. There were several cutoffs and a long S-bend.

Halfway through the bend, a red Austin mini met them. When the two cars were side by side, they halted. There wasn't room for the doors to be opened. Instead, the rear windows were rolled down.

"Through the window!" To the command was added a prod from the Webley.

Carter managed to crawl through. His legs had scarcely cleared when the mini lurched forward. It careened off the alley into one of the cutouts, and his new *galabiya*-clad seat companion, also with Webley, handed him a black hood.

"Put this on!"

Carter did.

"Now get down on the floorboard!"

He started to, and was helped along by powerful hands and the barrel of the gun.

When he was on the floorboard with the man's feet on his chest, the muzzle of the Webley stayed near his crotch.

"Do not try to look to see where we go, or try to see

my face. If you do, I will shoot. Not to kill, of course. Maybe I just shoot your cock off. Nod if you understand, Carter."

The Killmaster nodded vigorously, not only from the threat, but also from the pain caused by the prodding Webley.

But he also made a careful mental note of the tone and timbre of the man's voice.

When the time comes, he thought, *this son of a bitch is going to be the first one to get it.*

They kept the hood on him the entire time, but through sounds and his sense of smell Carter was able to pick up a few things.

The air was cleaner, hotter, and drier. That, plus the length of time they had driven, would place them quite a distance from the city center of Cairo, either in the hills or the western desert.

From the sounds, he guessed it was a small village teeming with tradesmen and children. He also guessed that they were somewhere near the river.

When they removed the hood, the room was so dim Carter didn't even have to blink to adjust his eyes.

There was only one window, and it was covered with a blanket. The only furniture was a long, rough-hewn table and two rattan chairs. It was stifling.

Carter was shoved into one of the chairs. The other, at the opposite end of the table, was occupied by a large, heavyset man naked to the waist. His legs in dirty white slacks were stretched out in front of him. His dark torso was glistening with sweat, either from the heat or the stone jug on the table in front of him. Beside the jug sat a machine pistol.

His head and face were covered with a burnoose.

There were four other men in the room, all in white *galabiyas* and burnooses.

Carter guessed they were the occupants of the two exchange cars.

"Do you want a drink?"

"No," Carter replied, "but I want my cigarettes."

The leader nodded, and one of the other men lit a cigarette and passed it to Carter. It was a harsh Egyptian brand.

"I can't have my own?"

"No. I don't trust your CIA. I have heard that you have poisoned darts in cigarettes and cigars."

Carter shrugged and inhaled the acrid smoke. "We are prepared to pay you a quarter of a million Egyptian pounds."

"No, a half-million . . . dollars."

"One hundred thousand . . . dollars."

"Ridiculous!" the man raged, grasping the machine pistol and cocking it as he aimed at Carter's chest. "I would kill you and be done with it now!"

Carter inhaled and blew two perfect smoke rings. They floated across the table unbroken in the still air.

"Yes, you could. But then you wouldn't get anything, would you?"

The tension lasted for a full three minutes. At last the man settled back in the chair. He dropped the gun to the table and drank from the jug.

"A quarter of a million American dollars."

Carter ground the cigarette out on the table and leaned forward on his elbows. "Koulami is using you."

"Koulami? . . . I know no Koulami."

"I think you do. I think his people kidnapped Donahue and turned him over to you."

"Why would this Koulami do that?"

"I haven't figured that out yet. Perhaps you did something for him and this ransom for Donahue is part of the payment. That's the way it usually works for mercenaries, isn't it?"

"Mercenaries! We are the People's—"

"Bullshit. You're a bunch of thieves trying to screw anybody you can."

The man's knuckles went white as he made two fists on the table. The tension in the room could be cut with a knife. Not one of them, even the leader, seemed to breathe.

Carter jumped on it.

"I want Donahue, but I also want Koulami. I'll tell you what I'll do. I'll give you one hundred thousand dollars for Donahue, and a half-million for both of them."

There were general grunts and groans, but there was no instant turn-down or acceptance of the offer.

"Wait."

Three of the men followed the leader from the room. Carter bummed another cigarette from the guard they had left behind, and waited.

It was nearly a half hour before they returned. Between two of them was Peter Donahue. He was doped, a little beat and battered and his clothes were in tatters, but he was breathing.

Carter wasn't too surprised when he got his answer.

"We know no Koulami. We accept the one hundred thousand American."

Carter shrugged. "So be it. Where and how do we make the trade?"

"It is now six o'clock. In six hours, at midnight—"

"No," Carter said.

"I told you, American, that we—"

"Would set the place, yes. *I* must set the time. It will take longer than that to get the cash." Now it was Carter's turn to buy the time he needed.

There was another hurried conference, this time in the far corner of the room. In the middle of it, the leader turned back to Carter.

"When? How much time will you need?"

"Until dawn tomorrow."

More talk.

"Very well, we make the exchange one hour before dawn tomorrow."

"Agreed."

"And we want the money in gold."

Carter hesitated for only a second. "That should be all right."

One of the men spread a map out in front of Carter. The leader had a similar map in front him that he referred to as he spoke.

"Do you see the area north of Cairo where the great Nile divides?"

"I do."

"You must get a white van. It must be white. Drive to the dam just before the divide. Cross the dam and wait until precisely six o'clock . . ."

That would be dawn, Carter thought.

"At precisely six, drive into the desert exactly four miles. There you will find a road to your right into the dunes. One mile into the dunes, stop and walk one mile further. Another van will meet you there, with Donahue in the rear. We will exchange vans. Anyone following you, or any helicopter overhead, and Donahue will be shot."

Carter concentrated on what he knew of the area. It was a good choice. Open country, but populous within a short distance. They could have a second van or car waiting, transfer the gold, and be gone without a trace.

If they weren't double-crossed.

Carter soon learned how they managed to cover that.

"There is a tearoom in the Khan bazaar. It is called the House of Abor. The woman, Eliza Brussman, will enter at exactly six o'clock. She will order breakfast and she will not leave until you receive my call. If she so much as rises to relieve herself before the call, she will be killed."

Neat, Carter thought, very neat.

At that time of morning the Khan el Khalili would be a teeming, shoulder-to-shoulder mass of humanity. Tradesmen and early-morning shoppers looking for the day's bargains would be as thick as flies on honey.

A person could be stabbed or shot in that mess and the assailant would be gone before the body fell down.

Carter agreed. "We have a bargain." He just hoped that Eliza would never have to take her morning breakfast in the House of Abor.

Four hours later, just after ten o'clock, Carter was dumped in a deserted street of the old quarter.

By the time he peeled off the hood, the only other living thing in the street was a mongrel dog whining and sniffing at his feet.

Film from the fifty and more cameras had already been collected by the time Carter grabbed a taxi and reached Government House. He, Effredge, and two of Najjar's people went over each print as it came out of the darkroom.

Abu Djabi's invisible street people had done a magnificent job. There were shots of Carter at every stage, and everyone around him had been included.

Carefully they culled through them, trying to get a pattern. By one o'clock in the morning, they had it.

Two men had spotted Carter at Tahrir Square. They were both in Bedouin dress, but the folds of their burnooses weren't over their faces. Again they were seen talking through the window of the red Austin. Again they were seen on two Vespas, obviously checking the rear of the Austin after the last switch was made.

"Looks like they may be small fry," Effredge said, "but they're the only obvious ones."

Carter nodded. "Their faces are the only clear ones. Let's hope somebody has a line on them. Get another set of these run off for Djabi."

Together, they walked the four best shots into Najjar's office. A runner was sent across town with a set for the fat old thief.

Najjar's computer came through with an ID almost simultaneously with the call from Djabi.

"The taller one with the scar across his nose is Hadi Rajdaq. He is very evil, my friend, a sadist. His chief pastime is raping and torturing young whores starving in the streets."

"An address?"

"My people tell me he shares a garret with another of his kind in the old city on the edge of the Muski. An alley called the Hareski. The other man might be the other in the picture."

"I would like three of your people to back us up, Abu. They will be paid well."

"I will send five for the price of three," the old man replied with a chuckle. "Hadi Rajdaq is a disgrace to our profession."

Carter hung up and turned to Najjar. The Egyptian was frowning over the man's picture and his criminal record.

"Well?" Carter asked.

Najjar leaned back and placed his hands at the back of his head. Carefully, with narrowed, unseeing eyes, he studied a crack in the plaster of the ceiling.

"Hadi Rajdaq is a festering pimple on the underbelly of Cairo."

That was all Carter needed. Carte blanche.

Hadi Rajdaq looked at the scene before him through hashish-dimmed eyes. After tomorrow he wouldn't have to be satisfied with street whores. He would have enough money to buy a dozen women of his own. He would make slaves of them, and for nothing they would do whatever he was pleased that they do . . . or endure.

He scratched himself and drooled a little as he watched his friend Bassa maul the young girl.

She was naked, and the man, Bassa, was stripped to the waist. From the perspiration covering their bodies, the struggle had been going on for some time.

The girl screamed as the man slammed her across the face with his open hand. He then pressed it over her mouth and, grinning wildly, forced her head back. He forced her body to his and bent his head to her small conical breasts. He got his lips around one of her breasts, and she sank her teeth into his hands.

Bassa bellowed with pain.

Rajdaq laughed softly.

The girl twisted out of the man's hands. He tried to hold her, but her sweat-drenched body was too slick. She ran toward the door, with Bassa directly behind her.

Halfway to the door, it burst from its hinges, splintering into the room. Carter came in, diving to the left. Effredge was directly behind him.

The girl screamed again and fell at Effredge's feet as the silenced Beretta barked twice, shutting off Bassa's roar.

Blood spread in a Rorschach pattern across the man's darkly matted chest, and he fell silent to the floor.

In his hashish delirium, Rajdaq whirled, trying to reach a holstered pistol hanging on the back of his chair. The barrel of Carter's Luger arced down, smashing the man's wrist.

At the same time, Effredge lifted the whimpering girl to her feet. "Get out!" he rasped in Arabic, and pushed her toward the door. One of the two dark figures in the hall hustled her away.

The door had barely closed behind her before Carter had Rajdaq spread on his belly across the table. Wordlessly, they went to work, one on each side of the man. Effredge planted a knee in the small of his back and held his left arm down while the fingers of his right hand curled in his greasy black hair. Carter held his right hand to the table, the butt of the Luger poised above it.

"Who has Donahue?" Effredge growled.

"You are both sons of whores and your mothers fuck pigs," Radjaq hissed.

Effredge lined Radjaq's face up with the table and broke his nose by crashing his face into the hard wood. For good measure, he slammed him two more times, and then turned the bloody pulp that was left up toward Carter.

"Who do you work for?" the Killmaster asked.

The man pursed his lips and spat blood into Carter's face. The Killmaster raised the Luger and brought the heavy butt down in a crunching blow across his hand.

"That's just for starters," Carter said. "I'll ask you one more time . . . who, and where. Every time you don't answer, I shoot another finger off."

They left him on the table, passed out, with two fingers remaining on his right hand, after he had answered each of their questions.

In the hall, Effredge mumbled in Arabic to Djabi's men.

Carter knew, as the two of them raced for the street, that neither of the men in the room behind them would see the sunrise.

If they hadn't had the exact location of the house, they would have spotted it from the van parked in the alley.

There was one man, dozing in the driver's seat, a machine pistol in his lap.

Carter took him out silently with Hugo.

At the end of the alley, Carter and Effredge climbed to the roof of a building and made their way back to the one they wanted.

Effredge went down the stairs from the roof. Carter took the fire escape.

The blanket was gone from the window now, and it was open to allow what little breeze there was into the room. Carter poked one eye around for a look.

The scene was almost as he had left it earlier. Saiad Muchasi was still stripped to the waist. He had discarded the burnoose. He was in the same chair, and a second man occupied the chair where Carter had sat.

The Killmaster heard a faint sound below him and looked down. Effredge was leaning out the window. He held up two fingers and then made a circle of his index finger and thumb.

He had taken out two men below, probably in the room with Donahue. One had gone in the van.

Muchasi and his greasy comrade were the only ones left.

"Aevno?" Muchasi wheezed, sipping from the jug.

"Yes, Saiad, it is time," the other man replied. "I will have them put the Britisher in the van."

Carter recognized the voice. The one called Aevno had been the one in the back of the Austin mini.

As he stood to leave, Carter shot him once in the middle of the forehead. Before the body had sprawled across the table, the Killmaster had tumbled through the window.

Muchasi made a lurching grab for the machine pistol on the table.

"Don't touch it," Carter hissed. "I want you alive."

FIFTEEN

Carter shook the sleep from his eyes and stretched in the bucket seat as the little jet touched down. The strip was military, in the desert south and east of Tel Aviv.

Muchasi was much more ready to talk than his people had been. Radjaq, compared to his leader, had been a lion. Muchasi started spilling his guts with just the threat that he was going to lose some fingers.

Two elements of his story dropped the last two pieces of the puzzle into place for Carter: the time period of seventy-two hours, and the arrangements for Koulam to pick up the ketch.

Now all he needed was absolute clarification and he had it.

They would need a special team, an extraordinary team, and there wasn't time to get them from the States. Delta Force, out of North Carolina, could have handled the job quite well. But they were halfway around the world.

A few high-level phone calls and the Israelis had

agreed to jump in with both feet.

Carter hoisted himself from the bucket seat the instant the plane came to a stop. A single man in combat fatigues, boots, and beret met him at the foot of the ladder.

"Carter?"

"Nick," the Killmaster replied, accepting the outstretched hand.

"I'm Major Zev Ben-Gal. I have a car waiting right over here."

"How are we set up and what do we know for sure?" Carter asked as they walked toward darkened buildings.

"Looks like all your suppositions were on the button. We've been in constant contact with one of your destroyers, the *Norman*, all day. The *Darvais Pride* is heading straight up the Persian Gulf, all right."

"And her course?"

"You were right there, too. She's drifting east little by little. Based on the timetable you gave us, she'll be on the fringe of Iranian waters by about eight tonight."

"So there's little doubt that she's not making any kind of direct heading toward Bahrain."

The major chuckled. "No doubt at all. She's playing with fire coming that close to the coast of Iran."

"What do your intelligence people say?"

"Nothing specific yet. Not enough to get a readout on."

Both men climbed into the back seat of the staff car. The driver sped away without receiving an order.

"Where are we headed?"

"We've set up communications at one of our southern bases outside Elat. We have a team and transport ready there if it's a go."

Carter sat back in the seat and smiled. "Oh, I have little doubt, Major, that it will be a go."

The base looked like little more than a large kibbutz in the desert north of Elat. On closer inspection, the buildings were disguised barracks, maintenance sheds, and hangars. A landing strip, impossible to spot from the air, had been laid down in the sand.

The nerve center was in an underground bunker.

Major Ben-Gal and Carter shot through security in seconds and were escorted into the most inner of the inner sanctums. There Carter met Colonel Isser Frank, who had been assigned to the project directly from Jerusalem.

Frank was a large man—large face, large hands, large feet. Everything about him projected size and strength. His face seemed devoid of expression, but his eyes—a deep, sparkling brown—were like those of a sage who had seen it all.

"You've got yourself a real knuckle-buster here, Carter."

The Killmaster nodded. "I wasn't thinking far enough ahead of them to start with, it seems. Koulami is sharp."

"Crafty is more like it," Frank growled, passing out coffee and leading them to a chart table. "I suppose Major Ben-Gal has told you we're in open-line communications with one of your destroyers?"

"He did."

"All right, their course is subtle right along here. Your people did two high flyovers, one at noon and another about fourteen hundred, an hour ago."

"Photos?" Carter asked.

The colonel spread out several fifteen-by-twenty glossies overlaid with light grid lines.

"Comparing your list of those aboard with these pictures, there are three more people on the *Darvais Pride* than there are supposed to be. Also, your list mentions only one woman, Quadima's wife. There are two other women on board."

"Do you have blowups?"

The colonel nodded and punched buttons on a console near his hand. The room darkened and a large wall screen came to life.

Carter narrowed his eyes and fidgeted as the pictures, made into black and white slides, appeared.

"Stop . . . that one!" He crossed the room, picked up a pointer, and touched it to the screen. "This part . . . magnify it!"

The colonel did, and Carter grunted. "This is Amin Koulami. The woman just behind him is Rami Sherif."

"You're sure?"

"I have no doubt of it."

The colonel sighed. "All right. Planning has come up with something we may be able to use."

Carter moved back to the table as Frank spread out a chart.

"We have three deep-cover people along the coast in Iran . . . from here to here. Yesterday, one of them reported an Iranian gun boat, the *Qualliah*, here in Bandar-e Chiru."

"Is that unusual?"

"Very. They don't usually patrol that area at all by sea. A reconnaissance flight once a day has always been enough because of the proximity to Oman and the United Arab Emirates. They don't want to take a chance on a boat-to-boat incident."

Carter leaned closer to the map, tracing the grid lines with his finger. With another finger he drew an imaginary line from Bandar-e Chiru out into the Persian Gulf.

"If my supposition that Koulami wanted to stall me with Donahue's kidnapping for seventy-two hours was correct, the *Darvais Pride* would be right about here at that hour."

"That's right," Major Ben-Gal said. "She would be just inside Iranian waters."

Carter cursed. "And if the gunboat *Qualliah* were here, she could intercept the *Darvais Pride* legally in her own waters."

Frank nodded. "It's a very crafty little plan. By the time all the diplomatic wrangling was over, Brussman's work would be done and Iran would have what she wants."

"And who knows," Ben-Gal added, "with the regime over there, everyone on the boat could be tried as spies and executed if it comes down to technicalities."

Carter stood and stretched. "So if all of our variables and guesses are correct, the only unanswered question is how the hell they hijacked the *Darvais Pride* in the first place."

"We might even have the answer to that, Carter," Frank said, punching the console again.

Carter moved to the screen as Koulami's arm and hand grew in size. The focus finally tuned in on a rectangular box in his hand. A handcufflike chain securely attached the box to his wrist.

"A radio-controlled detonation device?"

"We think so," Frank said. "Somewhere along the

line, probably in Alexandria, they mined the yacht.''

"And then made a suicide threat when they intercepted with the ketch," Carter hissed. "Give up or blow up."

"Our intelligence people see it that way," Ben-Gal replied.

Carter went back to the chart. "But if we could intercept the *Qualliah* before she intercepted the *Darvais Pride* . . ."

The major and the colonel exchanged looks and then smiled.

"Carter," Frank said, "are you suggesting that we commit piracy on the military craft of another nation?"

"That's exactly what I am suggesting," Carter said.

The smile on Frank's lips faded to a thin line. "And that's exactly what our planning ops people have come up with."

The flare arced into the sky, glowed a fiery red, and mellowed to orange as it dipped and fell into the sea. It had barely disappeared when Ben-Gal fired a second one and all hands peered across the sea toward the distant hulk of the gunboat *Qualliah*.

"She's taken the bait," the old man hissed. "She's turning this way."

"All right," Ben-Gal cried, "one man in the bow, one man aft, under the canvas! Carter, you under fallen sail, here. I'll be below. Judith . . ."

The young woman nodded, and without further orders shinnied up what was left of the main mast. It had been cracked in the middle, and the top half and the sails now draped over the port side amidships.

Carter slid under the sail and jacked a shell into the

chamber of an Uzi submachine gun.

It was a dangerous and daring plan, but it had every reason to work.

They had flown by unmarked plane into Bahrain posing as a team of bank auditors. Two U.S. helicopters had picked them up there.

The old man was an Iranian fisherman. He was also deep cover for the Mossad. He had set sail hours before from one of the many coastal islands north of Bandar-e Chiru.

One hour earlier, the team—Carter, Ben-Gal, the woman, Judith, and two agents—had dropped from the chopper to rendezvous with the old man and his fishing boat.

Now the old man stood at a useless tiller while Judith, masquerading as his daughter, had climbed the mast to inspect the break that had stranded them at sea.

Carter could hear the steady throb of the gunboat's engines. When he heard them idle back, he lifted a corner of the sail ever so slightly.

The *Qualliah* was pulling alongside, its twin lights bathing the fishing boat.

"What is the trouble?"

"Our mast snapped and my engine is out," the old man replied.

"Where is your port?"

"My daughter and I are fishermen out of Hendorabi. I have my license. Can you tow us?"

According to intelligence, there were five men aboard the gunboat: a radioman, an engineer, a skipper, and two hands.

Carter could see one man in the wheelhouse and three at the rail. The missing man was probably the engineer, somewhere below.

"We are on night patrol" came the answer. "We cannot tow you."

You mean you're on a timetable for a rendezvous and you can't take the time, Carter thought.

"Then, can you take my daughter and me on board?" the old man called.

There was a confab between the three men at the rail. At last one of them shouted back, "Yes, we can do that much."

Carter tensed. They had talked out the next few seconds a hundred times in the last three hours.

Judith went over first and then the old man. He produced his license and other documentation to the three men at the rail. The woman drifted behind them. Carter saw her hands fumbling at the small of her back beneath her heavy sweater.

Then he saw the glint of the pistol in her right hand as she darted into the wheelhouse. He heard the scrape of booted feet to his left, and then Ben-Gal's voice in Farsi:

"Stand fast! Don't move, any of you!"

Carter came out from under the sail and vaulted the rail, as did the two other agents. The fifth man, the engineer, was just emerging from the hatch when he found himself staring into the barrel of Carter's Uzi.

"This is piracy!" the *Qualliah*'s skipper finally managed to blurt.

"That's right," the major replied. "We're international terrorists."

"But what do you want?"

"The loan of your ship for a while, that is all."

The four hands were bound and gagged below. The skipper was taken into the wheelhouse.

"Now," Ben-Gal said, probing the man with his Uzi,

"we want your course for the intercept of the *Darvais Pride*, and we want your recognition signal."

"You're mad!"

"Very. You have one minute before I start killing your men."

Five minutes later they were on course for intercept.

Three hundred yards short of the *Darvais Pride*, the two powerful searchlights were flicked on. At the same time, Carter, in a hooded wet suit, slipped over the stern of the *Qualliah* with a towline attached to his belt.

Twice, as the gap between the two boats narrowed, he bobbed his head above the surface.

He recognized Jurgens, the yacht's skipper, at the rail, flanked by a woman and another man. There was a dark figure just aft of the wheelhouse and he saw movement inside, at the wheel.

Carter guessed this would be Koulami and the other woman.

If that were the case, the passengers and the rest of the yacht's crew would be locked below.

Just as the bow of the gunboat came level with the stern of the *Darvais Pride*, Carter dropped off.

He cut right and swam with all his might to get around to the vacant starboard side of the yacht before his lungs started screaming for air.

At last he surfaced. Two hard strokes took him amidships. He could hear voices from the port side, and then the gentle thud of the gunboat's rubber bumpers against the side of the yacht.

Wilhelmina was in an oilskin sheath, shoulder-rigged under his left armpit. He pulled himself far enough out of the water to unclip the Luger and slide Hugo between his teeth.

Then he grasped one of the rail uprights and slowly pulled himself upward until his eyes were just over the level of the deck.

The starboard side, as he'd hoped, was deserted. All attention was on the gunboat.

Cautiously, as silent as a cat, he got a toehold on the deck and swung himself over the rail.

He was two steps toward the wheelhouse when Rami Sherif stepped out. A sliver of light from one of the searchlights fell across her face.

She saw Carter instantly but seemed more curious than surprised. She took another step forward, and then her eyes grew wide. She had seen the wet suit and the hood.

Her lips parted, and Carter could see the throb in her throat as she started to scream out a warning.

The scream became a barely audible gargle as Hugo drove into her throat. Her hands went instinctively up to claw the pain from her neck. They had barely touched the stiletto's hilt when life left her.

Carter bolted forward. He caught her just as she started to fall and eased her silently to the deck. In practically the same flowing movement, he darted into the wheelhouse.

Thankfully, both portside windows had been pulled down. Carter stayed in the shadows, leaning forward only far enough to place everyone.

Judith and the old man were out of sight on the gunboat. Ben-Gal's two agents were arranged fore and aft on the lights. They had exchanged clothes with the crew.

The *Qualliah*'s skipper, with Ben-Gal at his shoulder, was amidships, talking over the rail to Captain Jurgens and the other two members of Koulami's team, a man and woman.

Both of them had machine pistols, and even though it looked as though they were buying everything so far, they had their guns at the ready with their fingers on the triggers.

Koulami himself was on the main deck just below Carter. He had moved twenty feet or so in front of the wheelhouse.

His thumbs were hooked in his belt, and the detonator box was hanging, swinging slightly, from his waist.

There was a flat, thin-lipped smile on his face, and his eyes gleamed like those of a cat in the light. The smile was smug, self-satisfied.

The Killmaster had two choices.

He could step from the wheelhouse and drop down on the man from above. That would entail getting him in one blow before he could reach for the box.

Or he could . . .

Carefully, Carter laid Wilhelmina's barrel over the lowered rim of the window. He gripped his right wrist with his left hand, sighted, and squeezed.

The 9mm slug caught Koulami dead center, left temple.

The right side of his head exploded and he fell like a rock.

Carter wheeled around, but there was no need.

Ben-Gal, before the roar from the Luger even peaked, had flattened the skipper of the *Qualliah*. In the same move he had reached across both rails and grabbed Jurgens. One hard yank had pulled the yacht's skipper over to the gunboat, where both of them fell in a heap on the deck.

Koulami's remaining two people lurched to the side, bringing their pistols into play.

But they were a millisecond late.

Ben-Gal's team was one of the best in the world, trained their entire lives for a situation just like this.

Judith came out of the *Qualliah*'s wheelhouse firing. The two agents at the lights joined in on the first burst.

Koulami's people were caught in a withering cross-fire. They were thrown across the deck before they could fire a shot.

Carter dropped to the deck as Ben-Gal stood.

"The fourth?" the Israeli asked. "The other woman?"

"Dead, port side," Carter replied, and headed for the hatch.

Out of the corner of his eye he could see the major barking at the gunboat's skipper.

He would be telling the man that this all happened in international waters. If he wanted to make an issue out of it, that would be fine.

Then the governments of Bahrain and Egypt would give the press the story and pictures, along with evidence that the government of Iran had stolen nuclear fuel and plutonium, and had engaged in piracy to abduct an English nuclear scientist.

Carter was pretty sure that by the time he got back on deck, the *Qualliah* would be hauling meekly back toward the coast of Iran.

He used Wilhelmina on the door of the main salon.

Quadima met him on the other side.

"It's over," Carter said. "You're all safe. We should be in Bahrain in less than three hours."

"Thank you. Thank you very much."

Josef Brussman appeared in the far hatch. "They said they had kidnapped my assistant, Peter Donahue. Is he all right?"

"He's fine, Dr. Brussman."

The man's shoulders sagged in relief. "Thank God."

"Don't you want to hear about your daughter, Doctor?"

"I assume Eliza can take care of herself," he replied stiffly.

"Yeah," Carter growled, "she sure can. She—and your son Peter—are on a flight to Rome. She said to tell you they'll wait for you there."

Brussman's face flushed beet red, but he managed a stiff nod of his head that served as a bow. "Thank you."

"Think nothing of it," Carter said, lighting a cigarette.

Brussman turned away.

"Doctor . . ."

"Yes?"

"I saved your ass, Doctor, but I would like the last word."

"Oh? And what is that?"

"I think you're a son of a bitch."

The Killmaster turned and climbed back up on deck.

The cigarette tasted bitter.

DON'T MISS THE NEXT NEW
NICK CARTER SPY THRILLER

THE MASTER ASSASSIN

As the sergeant stooped to enter his tent, the girl suddenly came alive. She attacked him viciously from behind, knocking him forward into the tent and collapsing the fragile structure.

Struggling noises came from beneath the walls of the tent, and Carter instinctively started to move in that direction. The Russian, however, held him off with a reassuring wave. "The sergeant can take care of himself," Revsky said, unaware that Carter's concern was for the girl.

In a few seconds Tiez emerged, holding a knife and dragging the girl by the wrist. Her face was cut on one side. A rivulet of blood oozed from her cheek and was seeping toward the corner of her mouth. Other than that, from what Carter could see, she wasn't badly hurt. Tiez, on the other hand, had nail marks on both sides of his forehead.

He was livid with anger. As he pulled her near the fire, his mouth twitched. Holding her down with one knee on her stomach, Tiez secured her wrists once more with what was left of the tether, then dragged her to the base of a nearby tree. The girl fought and her screams filled the air, but Tiez was oblivious to her struggles. He tied a knot in the end of the tether and wedged it between two branches of the tree, then he tore away the ragged animal-skin dress she wore.

She had a beautiful body, as smooth and lithe and muscular as a jungle cat.

The men didn't move. They were fascinated.

The sergeant pulled out his shirt and began to undo the buckle of his belt. The look on his face had changed from anger to grim determination, but Carter could see the anger was still there, smoldering underneath like a hayfire, ready to flare up at any moment. If the girl survived this ordeal, she wouldn't live long afterward. The sergeant was in a mood to kill.

Suddenly Carter knew he couldn't wait any longer. If he was going to make a move, it had to be now. He leaped at the sergeant, a high, arching karate kick that might well have split the man's head if Carter hadn't altered the angle slightly and come down in the middle of his back. Tiez flew off the girl and tumbled into a thicket of fern.

The girl didn't need any more chance than that. She sat up, and with a powerful yank, she pulled her hands free. Then, with her wrists still bound, she scrambled to her feet and darted into the trees. She looked like a gazelle, her tan buttocks pumping as her legs carried her to safety.

Tiez was on his feet in a second. He started after her but soon saw he was hopelessly outdistanced. Then he turned to Carter. His eyes burned like coals in his head, and his fists clenched and unclenched at his sides.

"Idiot!" he hissed. "What the hell do you think you're doing?"

"They're human beings," said Carter calmly, turning away. "You can't treat them like animals."

Tiez ran around to Carter's other side, thrusting his face up into Carter's. "What the hell do you know?" he yelled. "You've been in this jungle a few days and you're going to tell me how to treat Indians?"

Patterson clicked a cartridge into the breech of his Uzi, and the sound caused everyone to stop and look at him. "You know, Sarge," he said slowly, "I thought we should've killed this joker this morning. Wanna do it now?"

"Yeah," said Tiez, warming to the idea. His mouth fanned into a broad smile. "Maybe we should. Who's going to know?"

Carter had been watching Patterson, looking for an opening. Now, as the American mercenary turned to grin at Tiez, Carter seized the moment. He snatched the gun barrel in a movement almost too quick to see.

Patterson's reaction was to pull back, but Carter anticipated this. He let Patterson go, then yanked him suddenly forward. At this point Patterson could either let go of the gun, which would put it into Carter's hands—and give Carter the drop on everybody—or hold onto the gun, which would bring him on a dead run into Carter's left fist. Patterson chose the latter.

Because of the speed of Carter's initial move, he had time to rear back and put a little weight behind his punch. This, combined with the force of Patterson's forward motion, seemed to almost destroy the man's nose when it hit. The nostrils split and blood showered his uniform.

The man staggered. He fell to his knees, but he did not let go of the gun. It was as though his hands had not yet received the message the rest of his body was broadcasting.

As Carter reached for the gun, something hard slammed into the small of his back.

Carter fell to the ground and rolled over twice, almost spinning into the fire. He sprang to his feet and saw it was Gallegos who had kicked him.

The other men were now beginning to react. Velasquez, Revsky, and Gallegos were all moving in Carter's direction, while Tiez headed toward the tents. The other guns had been stacked there, and although the other three men were much closer and posed a more immediate threat, it was Tiez who worried Carter. Somehow the Killmaster had to keep the sergeant from reaching the weapons.

Gallegos had covered more ground than the others. He had followed his kick to Carter's back and was now within a few feet of Carter, looking for an opportunity to do more damage. But Carter was on his feet this time and facing him.

He feinted to his left, then went low, moving like lightning, sweeping the man's legs out from under him with a broad kick. Gallegos went down and Carter leaped on him with a punch to the rib cage that made the soldier's body jump as though it had received an electric shock.

Then came the other two.

Tiez, meanwhile, was at the guns, picking one up. Carter felt a new urgency to stop him.

The Russian was small, half a foot shorter than his Latino buddy, and weighed probably thirty pounds less. Carter sprang for him, arresting his forward motion b grabbing his clothes and picking him up bodily off the ground. Then, with one hand on his chest and the other on the belt of his pants, Carter hurled the young man back. Revsky flew into Tiez, who was just about to swing around with the gun. The two fell over each other, sprawling onto the ground and scattering the guns.

This left Velasquez, the Latino kid. He, too, had been carrying a gun earlier. He was the kind who was attracted to a gun in almost a sexual way. A gun to him was like a woman; he needed to have it close by to fondle and stroke. But when he had seen the fight ensuing, he had put the gun aside. He had also stood by and let Carter throw his Russian comrade a dozen feet through the air. He seemed very eager to confront Carter one-on-one, and as Carter turned to him, he quickly saw why. The boy had drawn himself into a karate stance and was circling, hissing like a cobra.

Carter immediately went into a fighting stance, very much aware that he had to dispose of this kid quickly before the others recovered. He didn't have time to spar.

He lashed out with another leg sweep, but it wasn't well timed. The kid skipped away, but not before delivering a sharp blow to Carter's knee. A flash of pain shot up Carter's leg.

Meanwhile, Gallegos had pulled himself up. He was still holding his bruised ribs, but he didn't look all that much worse for wear. Velasquez was about to charge from Carter's left. Gallegos now came in from the right.

But Carter was more than ready. The adrenaline in his system had taken him past the point of needing to think. He charged with a flurry of punches and kicks, spinning like a dervish. He caught Velasquez on the jaw, shot a knee into his stomach, and, as he was falling away, chopped the nerve center at the back of his neck. The man's body stiffened like a pole, then lay still on the ground, hovering near unconsciousness.

Simultaneously, the Killmaster attacked Gallegos. The man got a short, rapid punch to the face and a sweeping kick to the head, Carter's leg stretched to its limits. The blow caught the soldier squarely on the temple. He went down like a felled tree.

Patterson's gun lay near the fire. Carter dashed for it and scooped it up. Tiez, too, after shoving the Russian aside, had scrambled for a gun, and he'd also brought his up, but not as fast as Carter.

"Hold it right there, Tiez."

Tiez saw that he'd lost. His eyes grew cautious and the gun loosened in his hand.

"Drop it," ordered Carter.

Tiez let the gun fall. "Most impressive, señor," he said, a smile playing at the corners of his mouth. "You didn't learn that in Colombia."

"You'd be surprised what you can learn in Colombia. A man has to learn to take care of himself anywhere."

"Then a man must always watch his back."

Carter started to turn, when the cold finger of a gun barrel pressed against the back of his neck. Strong hands wrenched the machine gun from his grasp, then a figure walked past him and sauntered into the light of the fire. It was a man wearing an Australian bush hat, pulled low on one side. The face was angular and sharp, but there was softness about it at the jowl and around the mouth.

A man who liked his comforts, Carter decided.

The man threw the gun to Tiez, then turned to face

Carter. "You fight like a mother leopard. Who the hell are you?"

"My name's Phil Royce. Who are you?"

"I, my friend, am Colonel Anderson."

—From THE MASTER ASSASSIN
A New Nick Carter Spy Thriller
From Charter in November 1986

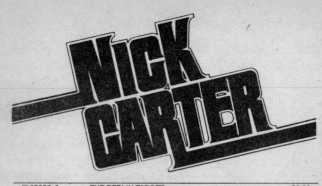

☐ 05386-6	THE BERLIN TARGET	$2.50
☐ 06790-5	BLOOD OF THE SCIMITAR	$2.50
☐ 57281-2	BLOOD ULTIMATUM	$2.50
☐ 06861-8	THE BLUE ICE AFFAIR	$2.50
☐ 57282-0	THE CYCLOPS CONSPIRACY	$2.50
☐ 14222-2	DEATH HAND PLAY	$2.50
☐ 57286-3	DEATH ORBIT	$2.50
☐ 21877-6	THE EXECUTION EXCHANGE	$2.50
☐ 57280-4	THE KILLING GROUND	$2.50
☐ 45520-4	THE KREMLIN KILL	$2.50
☐ 24089-5	LAST FLIGHT TO MOSCOW	$2.50
☐ 51353-0	THE MACAO MASSACRE	$2.50
☐ 52276-9	THE MAYAN CONNECTION	$2.50
☐ 52510-5	MERCENARY MOUNTAIN	$2.50
☐ 57502-1	NIGHT OF THE WARHEADS	$2.50
☐ 58612-0	THE NORMANDY CODE	$2.50
☐ 69180-3	PURSUIT OF THE EAGLE	$2.50
☐ 57284-7	THE SAMURAI KILL	$2.50
☐ 74965-8	SAN JUAN INFERNO	$2.50
☐ 79822-5	TARGET RED STAR	$2.50
☐ 79831-4	THE TARLOV CIPHER	$2.50
☐ 57285-5	TERROR TIMES TWO	$2.50
☐ 57283-9	TUNNEL FOR TRAITORS	$2.50

Available at your local bookstore or return this form to:

 CHARTER
THE BERKLEY PUBLISHING GROUP, Dept. B
390 Murray Hill Parkway, East Rutherford, NJ 07073

Please send me the titles checked above. I enclose _____ Include $1.00 for postage and handling if one book is ordered; 25¢ per book for two or more not to exceed $1.75. California, Illinois, New Jersey and Tennessee residents please add sales tax. Prices subject to change without notice and may be higher in Canada.

NAME_____

ADDRESS_____

CITY_____ STATE/ZIP_____

(Allow six weeks for delivery.)

A8